Other books by Margaret Ryan:

Operation Boyfriend
Operation Handsome
Operation Wedding

And for younger readers:

HOVER BOY:
1. Fizzy Feet
2. Beat the Bully
3. Missing Moggy Mystery

THE CANTERBURY TALES:
1. The Big Sister's Tale
2. The Little Brother's Tale
3. The Little Sister's Tale

Look out for more Kat McCrumble *books, coming soon!*

KAT McCRUMBLE

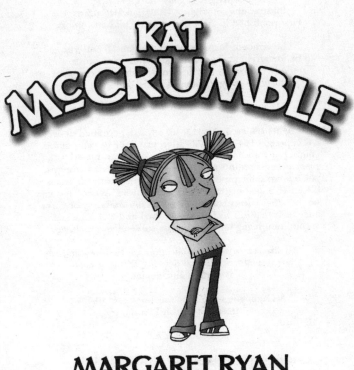

MARGARET RYAN

*Hodder
Children's
Books*

A division of Hodder Headline Limited

To Heather with love

Text copyright © 2004 Margaret Ryan
Illustrations copyright © 2004 Jan McCafferty
First published in 2004 by Hodder Children's Books

A Catalogue record for this book is available
from the British Library

ISBN 0 340 87827 4

Typeset in Baskerville by Avon DataSet Ltd,
Bidford-on-Avon, Warwickshire

Printed and bound in Great Britain by
Bookmarque Ltd, Croydon, Surrey

The paper and board used in this paperback are natural
recyclable products made from wood grown in sustainable
forests. The manufacturing processes conform to the
environmental regulations of the country of origin.

Hodder Children's Books
A division of Hodder Headline Limited
338 Euston Road
London NW1 3BH

Scottish for Beginners

Ben: mountain. As in, 'I'm off to climb Ben Nevis, I may be some time.'

Blether: to chat idly or foolishly. As in, 'Och, away and stop your blethering.' Would be said by your mother when you're desperately trying to convince her how much you really need new designer trainers because EVERYONE else in your class has them.

Ceilidh: pronounced 'KAYLAY'. An informal gathering with singing, dancing and perhaps storytelling. We like them.

Clootie dumpling: A dried fruit dumpling wrapped in a cloth and boiled. Yummy!

Clype: a tell-tale. We don't like them.

The Mod: Annual Gaelic festival of music and literature. Only good singers need apply. That lets me out.

Plaid: pronounced 'PLAD'. Rectangular length of woollen cloth usually in tartan. Now only worn as ceremonial dress by people in pipe bands, and daft folk at weddings.

Shooglie: wobbly, shaky, unsteady. As in, 'This table has a shooglie leg,' when your mince and potatoes slides on to your lap.

Stushie: uproar, unnecessary fuss. As in, the stushie your mother creates when you go ahead and buy those designer trainers.

Tablet: Scottish sweet, a little firmer than fudge. Seriously yummy. Seriously bad for the teeth. Nevertheless, see recipe at end of book.

Chapter 1

Hi, I'm Kat. Officially my birth certificate says I'm Katriona Mhairi McCrumble, but I'm Kat to my friends. Not Carrot Head, as some people call me. Though they don't call me that for long. I have the fiery temper to match the hair.

In my dreams, I'm beautiful, elegant and talented. In the mirror, I'm a bit scruffy and freckly like the rest of my family. I am surrounded by McCrumbles. There's a little bit of Scotland, on the west coast, just north of the Great Glen, where a lot of them hang out. Have done for centuries. Ever since Adam (McAdam?) was a lad. I live in the little village of Auchtertuie. I know that name looks a bit like a giant sneeze, but you can say it. Honest.

Try . . . OCH-TER-2-Y.

See. Easy.

Auchtertuie is a few miles away from Fort William, the nearest town, and hugs the winding edge of Loch Bracken. Behind the village is a huge forest which rises to cover the lower slopes of the dark and mysterious Ben. Slap bang in the middle of Auchtertuie, on the shore road facing the loch, is my home, the Crumbling Arms inn. I love the old inn, even if bits of it are falling down. I live there with my dad, Hector, and . . . well, before I go on, perhaps I'd better fill you in on some of the details of my family. I should warn you, they're not exactly normal.

I'll start with my dad. He's the best dad in the world: kind, thoughtful, generous with money – whenever he has any – but he's not all there. I don't mean that bits of him are missing – or perhaps I do, because he seems to have mislaid his memory. Like he put it down some place and can't remember where. Sometimes he's so forgetful I threaten to sew a name tag on to his favourite old jersey, in case one day he forgets who he is. But he'd probably take off the jersey and lose it. Maybe a tattoo on his arm would be better.

Then there's Kirsty McCrumble, our cook at the Crumbling Arms. She's a cousin of Dad's, twice removed. Removed from reality when she's been at the malt whisky. She keeps a bottle on the kitchen dresser inside a big blue and white jar marked 'Flour'. She says the whisky's purely for medicinal purposes. So, when I hear 'Scotland the Brave' being sung off-key, and see Kirsty marching up and down the kitchen twirling the broom handle like a pipe band major, I know she's been taking her medicine. But she's still the best cook north of the Great Glen.

I mustn't forget Donald, our handyman. As if. He's a distant relative too, and a druid. Part time. When he's not trying to patch together crumbling bits of the Crumbling Arms, he's up a tree somewhere. Trees are very important to druids. They consider that whatever grows on them is a gift from heaven, like mistletoe at Christmas. So Donald spends a lot of time with trees: talking to them, hugging them or just sitting in them.

Local folks are used to his funny little ways, but tourists sometimes get a fright when a man in a white frock suddenly leaps down from above. But Donald wouldn't hurt a fly. The tourists usually end up taking his photograph. Sometimes, if he likes them, he gives them a blessing. They like that. Sometimes they give him money. He likes that. He uses it to buy more trees.

Finally, there's Morag McCrumble, our postie. I think she's related to everyone round about. Everyone knows Morag. Not just because she delivers their mail, and their rolls and milk too if they're poorly, but because she has the 'second sight'. She 'sees' things the rest of us can't. When she 'sees' things, she gets a faraway look in her eye – the blue one I think it is, the other one's amber – and her voice goes funny, like it's coming out of a long tunnel. She can tell you what's in your mail before you've even opened it. Weird or what?

'Not good news, Hector,' she said to Dad one morning, before he'd had a chance to open the letter demanding more money for the rates.

'Good news, Kat,' she said to me, when she handed me a letter saying I'd won first prize in a painting competition.

Some people think that having the 'second sight' is a lot of nonsense, but others come from miles around to consult Morag. They want to know things like, should they marry their current boyfriend or will their football team win the league. Sometimes she can help them, other times she tells them to go away and not be so daft.

But she's daft on my dad. Fancies him like mad. That's why she spends so much time at the Crumbling Arms. But Dad never notices. He just smiles and says 'Thank you, Morag,' when she's single-handedly dug out a huge tree-stump from our back yard, or chopped us enough logs to last a lifetime. And 'Thank you very much, Morag,' when she's helped build and repair the runs and pens we have in the back yard.

You see, although running the Crumbling Arms is our business, Dad and I really want to set up a proper wildlife sanctuary at the back of the inn. We have plenty of room, but it's an expensive thing to do. The inn doesn't make much money, so we have to try to save up as best we can. With our home-made runs and pens, we already look after distressed animals that are brought to us. We had a sparrow-hawk with an injured wing the other week. We think he was probably struck by a car. But, with a bit of rest and looking after, he was soon as good as new, and we released him back into the wild. That's the really great bit, seeing a bird fly free again.

We get lots of hedgehogs too. Kamikaze hedgehogs. They have absolutely no road sense. Never heard of looking both ways. Never heard of waiting for the Green Man. I'd like to set up special hedgehog crossings. They'd be like zebra crossings, but with little hedgehogs painted on the white stripes. I would paint them myself, if the council would let me. Perhaps I'll just sneak out one night and do it anyway. There's a little bit of road just outside Auchtertuie that would be perfect.

We would like to be able to treat more injured animals, but until we have better facilities it's very difficult. Still, we do the best we can, and Morag's a great help.

That's my family, then: me, Kat McCrumble; my dad, Hector; and the people who help in the Crumbling Arms. But that's only my human family. I haven't told you yet about my animal one.

Chapter 2

We've always had pets at the Crumbling Arms, ever since I can remember. Dad is an animal lover and my mum was too. I don't remember much about my mum – she died when I was little – but I have a photo of her I keep on my bedside table. She was very pretty. I hope I grow up to look like her, but I probably won't. I take after my dad's side of the family. I've told you about the red hair and the temper. I try to control my temper, but sometimes it just gets the better of me, especially where animal cruelty is concerned. Then I go ballistic in a big way.

Do you know that Donk, our rescue donkey, had been so ill treated that his head collar was imbedded about three centimetres into his face? It was right through to the bone and so tight he couldn't open his mouth properly to eat. He had wasted away to a rickle of bones. How can people treat animals like that? I'd like to put Donk's former owner in a tight head collar and see how he liked it. See, temper. I know. But cruelty to animals makes me so angry.

Anyway, the owner was prosecuted and Donk was rehomed with us. His poor old nose looks a bit odd after the operation to remove the head collar, but he has the loveliest, saddest eyes you've ever seen. He's still a little bit wary of strangers, but he's one of my best friends. I go out to the back yard and talk to him every day, especially if I'm feeling low, or annoyed about something. He's a very good listener. He nuzzles my cheek with his nose and licks my ear. I think it's the donkey equivalent of a cuddle. It's lovely, and works every time to cheer me up.

Two of my other best friends are Millie and Max. They are mother and son Border collies. Millie is sane and sensible and orderly in her ways. Max is a lunatic. They belonged to Dougal McDougall, who had a sheep farm a few miles inland from Auchtertuie. Dougal was quite old and needed to retire. There were no relatives to take on the farm so Dougal sold it and went to live with his married daughter in Glasgow. But a top-floor flat in a big city tenement is no place for two sheepdogs, used to roaming the hills. So Dougal asked if we'd take them. Of course we said yes. They'd been coming to the inn with Dougal for years anyway for Kirsty's fine dinners, and we knew them well.

Millie does her best to keep Max in order, but it's not easy. Max has never quite learned the difference between humans and sheep, and sometimes rounds up all the guests in the Crumbling Arms and herds them into a corner. Then he stalks them to make sure they stay in a tight bunch, and that no strays manage to escape. When he's happy with them, he sits back on his haunches with his pink tongue hanging out, and a 'well done me' expression on his face.

Then Dad has to apologise to the guests and give them all free drinks to make up for Max's behaviour. No wonder the Crumbling Arms never makes much money!

The inn wouldn't be complete without Samantha, our Siamese cat. Nobody knows where she came from. One minute we didn't have a cat, the next minute we did. She appeared at the inn out of nowhere. No one saw her arrive. We asked round about if anyone had lost her. Morag asked everyone on her rounds too. We put a notice in the post

9

office window. We put a notice in the local paper. We even put a notice in a national paper. Nothing. No one came forward to claim a rather superior Siamese cat wearing a blue collar to match her eyes. The new disk on the collar said 'Samantha', nothing more. She's still a mystery. She won't answer to Sam, only Samantha, and then only if she's in a good mood. We wondered if she'd been let out of a car which had gone off and left her. Who knows? Only Samantha, and she's not telling. Anyway, we love her, and she puts up with us.

And that's all the pets except for Flip, and he's not really a pet at all. He's our visiting badger. The Gaelic name for badger is Brock, but we call him Flip because he flips open the cat flap in the kitchen door and pokes his black and white stripey head through. If he thinks it's safe, he squeezes in the rest of himself, and eats Samantha's cat food. Chicken liver's his favourite. He and I have become best friends over the years. He lets me feed him if I'm in the kitchen when he arrives. Then he turns tail and leaves the way he came in.

I managed to follow him once, back to his sett in the forest. I returned later that night with Dad to see if I could spot him again, and I did. When the light started to fade he poked his nose out of the sett, decided it was safe, and brought out his family.

They had a great time snuffling around and playing roly-poly with each other. We watched until it was dark, then we slipped away. Magic.

Now Flip comes for his cat food almost every night. Probably leaves Mrs Flip to cope with the kids. Probably says, 'Cheerio, dear, I'm just off to the pub!'

So that's my animal family. Now that it's the summer holidays, we'll be getting more animals to look after while their owners are away. We get the usual run of cats and dogs, rabbits and guinea pigs; though Emily, the tarantula, generally comes to board about now, too. She looks a bit hairy and scary, but really she's a big softie, and no bother at all.

So, I was looking forward to a pleasant summer. No more boring lessons for a while, no piles of homework, no hassle, I thought.

Just how wrong can one girl be?

Chapter 3

When you waken up in the morning you never really know what the day's going to bring, do you? It might bring a letter saying you've won a fortune. It might bring a long-lost auntie to stay. Or, it might bring a phone call from your teacher to ask why you're not at school. I only dodged school once. Honest. It was late last spring, and there was a female otter I'd been keeping an eye on, about to bring her two new cubs down to the lochside for the first time. I couldn't miss that. I deliberately missed the school bus, which stops at the chippy further along the shore road, and sneaked away to my hiding place behind a large rock on the lochside.

I sat there on my rucksack, watching and waiting, nibbling on my packed lunch. I was just trying to crunch my crisps as quietly as I could when Ma Otter appeared at the top of a nearby rocky outcrop. She looked about, sniffed the air, then led her two cubs down from their holt, to the water's edge. It was a fine sunny day and the deep waters of the loch sparkled invitingly, but the cubs were unimpressed. Otter cubs don't take naturally to water, and this pair were no exception.

Ma Otter tried to coax them in.

'Come on, little fellows, in you go, the water's fine.'

'Don't want to.' And they hung back.

Ma Otter tried to push them in.

'Now, don't be so silly. Just jump in.'

'You jump in if you want to. We're staying here.'

These were serious landlubber cubs.

Finally Ma Otter got fed up with them. She lifted them up in her mouth, went to the water's edge and dunked them! Boy, were they surprised! But they quickly got used to it.

'Hey, look at me, Mum. I can dive deeper than him.'

'Oh no you can't. Watch me, Mum. I'm best.'

Wouldn't you have preferred that to isosceles

triangles and media studies? Yep, me too. I had a fantastic day.

It wasn't quite so fantastic though when Dad found out I hadn't been at school. That's one of the disadvantages of living in a small community, everyone knows what you're up to!

Dad gave me a severe talking-to. 'School is important, Kat,' he said. 'If you don't pass your exams, how will you get to vet school? How will you be able to look after the sick animals when we've got our wildlife sanctuary?'

I examined the toes of my trainers. I knew he was right. But these otter cubs had been something special.

'Tell me all about the cubs, then,' said Dad after a moment, and that was the severe talking-to over. Phew.

In Auchtertuie you never know what the weather's going to be like either. The locals say, if you can see the top of Ben Bracken, it's going to rain, and if you can't, it's raining already. We can have all four seasons in one day here, so everyone wears layers of clothing that can be removed if necessary. Only Donald in his druid's frock never seems to notice the weather.

That first morning of the school holidays, I got up, put on my usual jeans, T-shirt and sweatshirt, and headed downstairs. It was 6.45 a.m. You probably like to sleep late in the holidays, and I do too, but Kirsty doesn't come in till ten, and if we have guests, there are breakfasts to do.

During term time Dad does his best to manage on his own, but that can be a disaster. He's not very good at doing two things at once, and with his memory . . . He's not too bad if someone just asks for porridge or bacon. But, porridge AND bacon? No chance. It wouldn't be the first time he's put the bacon in the pot and the porridge under the grill. And what if the guests want toast as well? The toaster's ancient. Dad keeps meaning to replace it, but forgets. The smoke from the toaster sets off the smoke alarm. The smoke alarm's a bit eccentric and won't stop until Dad gets out the stepladder, climbs up and taps it three times with Kirsty's toffee hammer. So, you can see why, when we have guests, it's easier to get up at 6.45 a.m. and help with the breakfasts.

That morning we had two ramblers and a twitcher. The ramblers, a jolly couple in matching Fair Isle jumpers, were looking out of the dining-room window when I arrived.

'What's the weather going to do today, Kat?' they asked.

I joined them at the window. I could see the top of the Ben.

'Better take your anoraks,' I grinned, and took their breakfast order. They wanted porridge, bacon, egg and tomato with a fried potato scone and some tea and toast. Help! Dad would never have coped.

I quite like to cook. Kirsty always let me 'help' in the kitchen when I was little, though my first attempt at fairy cakes was a disaster. There was more flour on me and on the floor than in the bowl, and, when the cakes were finally ready and I carried them proudly to my dad, I left ghostly white footprints all over the inn.

Actually we do have a ghost. I nearly said a real live ghost, but you know what I mean. He's called Old Hamish and I've seen him several times, but I'll tell you more about him later.

'You do the porridge, Dad,' I said when I took the ramblers' order to the kitchen. 'And be careful not to burn it.'

Dad did his best to look affronted. 'Have I ever been known to burn porridge?' he asked.

'Yes.'

'Fair enough,' he grinned, and measured out the ingredients. Oats, milk or water, and salt is the Scottish way of making porridge.

By the time the ramblers had finished their porridge, I was ready with the rest of their breakfast. Then I breathed a sigh of relief till the twitcher appeared.

You know how it's sometimes said that people get to resemble their pets? Well, there may be some truth in that because our twitcher definitely had a kind of birdlike appearance. Bit of a beaky conk flanked by black feathery eyebrows. He also had a way of nodding his head like an excited budgie. And, guess what he wanted for breakfast? Muesli with extra sunflower seeds, if we had them. I raided Kirsty's larder, and mixed him up a large bowlful. Then he went off whistling, to look for golden eagles.

Dad and I had just cleared away and sat down at the kitchen table with our tea and toast when Morag arrived. She came in by the back door, accompanied by Millie and Max, who know she always keeps a doggy treat for them in her pocket.

'Sit,' she told them, as she put down her postbag and reached into her jacket.

Millie obediently sat. Max bounced up and down like he was on springs.

'The dog's deaf,' smiled Dad.

'No, daft,' I grinned.

Morag shook her head and doled out the doggy

treats before tickling the collies' tummies. Then she smiled at Dad and rummaged in her bag for his mail. She took out a letter and handed it to him. Her eye, the blue one, took on its faraway look and she frowned.

'I'm afraid it's not good news, Hector,' she said.

Chapter 4

Dad looked at the letter. There was nothing on the outside of the plain white envelope to indicate bad news. No mysterious black spot, no ominous red cross, not even the stamp stuck on upside down. And the address label was neatly typed.

Dad shrugged and was just opening the letter when Kirsty and Donald arrived. They took one look at Morag's solemn face, the letter in Dad's hand, and waited quietly. I waited too. If there was bad news, it was family business, and the family were present. Dad took out a single sheet of paper and started to read. The expression on his face went from complete surprise to total incredulity.

'I don't believe it,' he said. 'It's from C.P. Associates. They want to buy the Crumbling Arms.'

'Whaaaat!' You could have heard the rest of us yell from the other side of Loch Bracken.

'B-B-B-buy the-the Crumbling Arms?' I stuttered. 'How ridiculous! Why would they want the Crumbling Arms? They've got their own enormous hotel on the big estate, is that not enough? Of all the cheek . . . I've got a good mind to go up to the estate office right now and tell them exactly what I think of their letter. Tell them to keep their greedy paws off the Crumbling Arms!' And I could feel my face getting as red as my hair.

Dad patted my hand. 'Calm down, Kat, calm down. The Crumbling Arms is our home and not for sale. Here, read the letter for yourself.' Dad handed it to me, and Morag, Kirsty and Donald crowded round.

'I knew no good would come of it when that lot bought the estate,' said Morag. 'I said so at the time.'

'Probably thought they could put us out of business with their luxury hotel and its fancy ways,' said Kirsty.

'But they reckoned without your cooking, Kirsty,' said Donald.

'And Kat's breakfasts,' smiled Kirsty, giving me a hug.

'So, what are we going to do?' I asked. 'Why do C.P. Associates want the inn? Why did they offer such a miserable sum for it? They must surely have known we'd refuse. I don't like this. They're up to something.'

Perhaps I should explain a bit about C.P. Associates, not that I know very much myself. I know that they're a big firm of international developers who bought the large estate that spreads out for miles behind Auchtertuie. The whole area used to belong to the McCrumble clan, but that was long ago when Old Hamish, our ghost, was alive. Now it belongs to C.P. Associates, who put in a new road and cleared some of the forest to build a glitzy, five-star hotel.

While it was being built I used to slip through the estate to have a sneaky look. The hotel has lots of bedrooms with en suite shiny white loos with gold fittings. The public rooms are enormous – big enough to hold a conference or a ball in. And the foyer is very impressive. You could just imagine Prince Charming coming down the great curving staircase, his long, jewelled sword clanking off the marble steps. The whole place is full of squashy sofas, antique carpets, and flower arrangements big enough to hide behind. (Now how would I know that, do you think?)

They also have an arcade with tiny little shops. Not Auchtertuie-type shops like Jinty McCrumble's bakery or James Ross's butcher's, but really posh shops with snooty assistants who wear bright green eyeshadow and very dangly earrings. The clothes in the shops cost nearly as much as it did to get our roof fixed last winter. Leading on from the arcade is a spa where, for a large fee, you can have your face steamed, your wrinkles ironed and your body covered in mud. I can get covered in mud every day for nothing by going out into our back yard to visit Donk.

I've never met C.P. Associates. Haven't even seen them, or him, or her. But I have met the head gamekeeper, Ron Jackson, who looks after the estate. I don't like him much, and it's not just because he found me hiding behind the large flower arrangement in the hotel foyer and threw me out. There's just something about him I don't trust. Millie and Max don't like him either. He sometimes comes into the bar of the Crumbling Arms in the evening and Millie and Max avoid him. That's really strange because they talk to everybody.

Ron Jackson manages the game on the estate so that the hotel guests can hunt and fish and shoot, if they like, and he's always on about how the wildlife, golden eagles, foxes etc, pinch his game. HIS game.

Doesn't he know the wildlife were there first, that they have to eat, the same as the rest of us?

Temper, Kat, temper!

But what makes me even more angry than Ron Jackson are the badger baiters. They operate from time to time in various parts of Scotland, and we've just heard a rumour that a group of them may be headed in our direction. May, in fact, already be here, operating right now with a team of terriers. Do you know what badger baiters do? They send the dogs down into the badger setts to flush the badgers out. Then they watch while the badgers and the terriers tear each other apart, fighting for survival. Can you imagine anyone getting pleasure from that? How sick can these people be? It makes my blood boil just to think about it. I expect you can tell! I visit the setts on the estate regularly just to check they're all right. Ron Jackson nearly caught me once, but I hid behind a tree. Fortunately it was bigger than the flower arrangement!

I folded up the letter and gave it back to Dad. 'What are you going to do?' I asked.

'Don't even bother to reply to that letter, Hector,' said Kirsty, banging pots about on the stove, a sure sign that she was agitated. 'Tear it up and file it in the bin.'

'Treat it with the contempt it deserves,' agreed Donald. 'The nerve of these people!'

'No, no,' said Dad. 'There's no need to be rude. I shall just write them a polite letter stating that the Crumbling Arms is not for sale.'

'Oh, Hector,' sighed Morag. 'You're far too nice to be a McCrumble.'

'Oh, Dad,' I said. 'Couldn't we at least get Donald to put an ancient curse on the letter before you send it?'

'But I don't do curses. Ancient or otherwise,' protested Donald. 'I only do blessings.'

'Couldn't you do a blessing backwards, then?' I said. 'I read about that somewhere and it's worth a try.'

'You're a fierce McCrumble, Kat,' laughed Dad. 'No doubt about that. But there will be no rudeness and no curses, backwards *or* forwards. I shall write to C.P. Associates declining their offer, and that will be an end of it.'

Just how wrong can one dad be?

Chapter 5

I promised to tell you more about our ghost, Old Hamish, didn't I? Well, the first time I saw him, he was standing at the top of the stairs inside the Crumbling Arms.

It had been an ordinary winter's evening in the bar. Dad was serving the few locals who had braved the biting wind to come out for a drink and a blether. I was in my bedroom doing my homework. Sort of. Actually, I was throwing a ball for Max, trying to teach him to catch it and bring it back. Max could catch it all right, but bringing it back was a problem. He rather liked the taste of old tennis ball and decided to keep it. We were just playing tug of war with it when my bedroom door flew open. Millie stood up, immediately alert. Max carried on tugging. There would have to be an earthquake before he would give up that ball, so I let go. A surprised, but pleased, Max fell back on to the carpet. I went towards the door.

'It's OK, Millie,' I said. 'It's only the wind. Someone must have opened the front door and the draught has funnelled up the stairs.'

But Millie wasn't happy. Her ears went back and she gave a little low moan in her throat.

'Look,' I said, going out into the hallway. 'There's nobody there. See.'

But there was. Hovering at the top of the stairs was an old man. He had long grey hair and was dressed in an old-fashioned McCrumble tartan kilt. A plaid, fastened with a heavy silver brooch, was thrown over one shoulder, and his white shirt was crumpled and worn. He seemed a bit lost, so I thought he must be looking for the loo.

'The public toilets are downstairs,' I said. 'Just to the right of the bar. The gents' has the little man in trousers sign on it,' I added, just in case his kilt confused him.

The old man nodded, smiled and disappeared.

I went back into my bedroom.

'Good girl, Millie,' I said, fondling her silky ears. 'You were right. There was someone there, but now he's gone. AAARGH! He didn't just go, Millie, he vanished completely! Help! DAAAAAD!'

Dad came bounding up the stairs two at a time. 'What's wrong, Kat, what's wrong? You're as white as a sheet. You look as though you've seen a ghost.'

That wasn't funny.

'Was there a stranger in the bar tonight?' I asked shakily.

'No,' said Dad. 'Why?'

I shook my head. 'There wasn't an old man with long grey hair wearing an old McCrumble tartan kilt and plaid?'

'No,' said Dad again. 'Why?'

'Are you sure?'

'My memory's not that bad, Kat. What *is* going on?'

'I think I've just seen Old Hamish!'

'Oh.' Dad sounded sceptical. He's not really into the supernatural. There are perfectly reasonable explanations for everything, he says. We just haven't found all of them yet.

'If you don't believe I saw Old Hamish, ask Millie,' I insisted.

Millie looked at both of us then came and rubbed her head on my leg. All that could be seen of Max was his rear end. The rest of him was under my bed searching for the ball that had rolled there. He obviously didn't believe in ghosts either.

'Something's certainly frightened you,' said Dad, putting his arm round me.

'I wasn't frightened,' I protested. 'Not at first. I spoke to him.'

'What did you say?'

'I told him where the loos were.'

Dad smiled, and, do you know, he looked a bit like Old Hamish. Just not as much hair or tartan.

'Stay here with Millie and Max,' said Dad, 'while I check the inn for any intruders.'

I nodded, but I knew that would be useless. I was sure I had seen Old Hamish, and he wasn't an intruder, he belonged here.

You see, the Crumbling Arms is built on the site of the original McCrumble castle. Old Hamish and his twin brother, Callum, lived in the castle and worked the land. At least, Hamish did. Callum spent the money. Legend has it that Callum liked fine clothes, fine wine and fine horses, and while Hamish was doing his best to look after the land and the people on it, Callum was off gallivanting. Eventually there was no money left, and Callum disappeared, leaving Hamish with a pile of debts. Hamish worked hard to pay them off. Keeping the McCrumble good name was very important to him.

But he couldn't pay the debts *and* make the necessary repairs to the castle. It fell into disrepair, then ruin. Old Hamish died penniless, still hoping for the safe return of his twin brother.

Years later, the Crumbling Arms was built by another McCrumble on the site of the old castle, using the same old stones. There have been McCrumbles at the inn ever since. So you can see why I didn't think Dad would find an intruder. It was only Old Hamish wandering about his old home.

I was right. Dad found no one. He phoned Constable Ross – James Ross the butcher's son – and asked him if there were any strangers in Auchtertuie that night.

'At this time of year?' said Constable Ross. 'I don't think so, not if they have any sense. That wind coming across the loch would cut you in two. But I'll check anyway.'

There was no one, and when everyone in Auchtertuie heard what had happened, they were all of one opinion.

'Kat McCrumble saw the ghost of Old Hamish.'

I've seen him several times since then. Usually on stormy nights. I wonder if he gets frightened. Can a ghost get frightened? So now I know if my bedroom door suddenly flies open, it could be the wind, or it could be Old Hamish. I've spoken to him again, to ask him what he wants – obviously not the loo! But he just smiles his kindly smile and disappears. Perhaps he just wants me to know he's there.

Chapter 6

Our ramblers and our twitcher moved on and some other guests arrived at the Crumbling Arms. The booking had been made some time ago in the name of McCrumble. We weren't surprised. We often get people, from all over the world, coming in search of their McCrumble ancestors. Some of them have even worked out their family tree. I tried to do that too, but my tree has lots of branches missing. Sometimes the visiting McCrumbles are really nice and invite me to go home with them for a holiday. I might just do that one day.

We knew our latest guests had arrived when we heard Ali McAlly's (real name Alistair McAllister) old taxi bang and clatter its way to a halt outside the front door.

'New arrivals,' said Kirsty. 'I'll put some tea and shortbread in the lounge for them.'

'Fine,' I smiled, and pinched a couple of the freshly made biscuits from the wire rack on the kitchen table. Dad was busy on the phone to the brewery – the delivery lorry was late again – so I went outside to greet the new guests. There were three of them: a man, a woman and a boy who looked about my age. They got out of Ali McAlly's taxi looking a little pale and shaky.

'Hullo, Kat,' said Ali, giving me the full benefit of his toothless smile. He has dentures, but likes to keep them for best. Only wears them on special occasions, like weddings or funerals. 'I've brought you your guests safe and sound.'

'Safe and sound!' screeched the woman, a vision in a scarlet top and shorts with matching shoes and lipstick. 'I've never been so terrified in my entire life!'

'Ach, just a few sheep on the road, Kat.' Ali winked at me. 'Had to swerve a couple of times to avoid them.'

'Don't you people have any straight roads in this country?' Scarlet mouth was yacking again. 'The sign at the station said "Auchtertuie four miles", but it took us forever to get here. I bet the cab driver went the long way round just to charge us more. Don't pay him, Roderick.'

'But there is only one way from the station,' I protested. Ali might fancy himself as a racing driver, but he was honest.

'Oh, never mind Beachbabe. She gets sick on the kiddie-go-round at the pleasure beach back home,' said the man, holding out his hand to me. 'I'm Roderick James McCrumble, the third, and this here's my son, R.J. the fourth. That there's my fifth wife, Beachbabe.'

'I'm Kat,' I said, shaking his hand. 'Kat McCrumble. Welcome to the Crumbling Arms. Kirsty, our cook, has put out some tea and shortbread for you in the lounge. Perhaps that'll help you recover from your journey.' And I gave Ali a sly wink.

'Tea? Don't you have any Diet Coke?' asked Beachbabe. 'And I never eat any kind of bread, it's so fattening.'

I looked at Beachbabe's tall skinny frame with its scarlet outfit and it reminded me of something. Got it! It was the old-fashioned red and white barber's pole on the wall outside Mario McCrumble's 'Cut an' Curl'.

'We'd love some tea and shortbread,' soothed the elder male McCrumble. 'Wouldn't we, R.J.?'

R.J. grunted something inaudible and thrust his hands deep into the pockets of his McCrumble tartan trousers. They were a funny length. I couldn't decide if they were long shorts or short longs.

R.J. saw me looking at them. 'Cool outfit,' I grinned.

R.J. looked at my ancient Levis and grunted again.

'Our trews are McCrumble tartan,' said his dad, as if I wouldn't know. 'I had several pairs made for both of us. I wanted us to blend in.' Then he looked along the street at the passers-by. There was a distinct lack of tartan.

'Don't you all wear the McCrumble tartan round here?'

'Not really,' I said. 'You'll see some kilts, but most folks just wear them for weddings or ceilidhs. Er, that's a kind of big Scottish party with dancing and singing.'

By this time Ali McAlly had got all their luggage out of the boot of his car and deposited it on the road. I went to help bring it in. There was a great deal of it, most of it belonging to Beachbabe, judging by the labels. She must have brought a lot of shorts.

'Be very careful with my bag,' she said, as I made to pick up a suitcase. 'Don't drop it.'

Drop it? I could hardly lift it.

'Let me help you with it,' offered R.J., and together we half carried, half dragged the suitcase into the inn. Then Donald dropped down from a nearby tree to help with the rest.

'Welcome to Auchtertuie,' smiled Donald, lifting the cases with ease. 'I'm Donald the druid.'

The new guests opened their mouths to say something then closed them again. I don't suppose they met many druids.

When everything was taken inside, the little hall of the Crumbling Arms held more luggage than people. Dad finished his phone call and beamed at the new arrivals from behind the reception desk. Actually, reception desk sounds a bit posh; it's really an old pine table that we unearthed from one of the outhouses in the back yard. Donald sanded it down and I painted purple thistles on it; their jagged green leaves spill down from the top on to the legs. Dad thinks it looks great.

'Gives the hall a bit of character, Kat,' he says.

Now he was chatting to the new guests. 'Wonderful to see some more McCrumbles,' he said. 'And all the way from the USA. I've put you in the two front bedrooms, facing the loch. They have the best view.'

Beachbabe leaned over the table and practically snatched the bedroom keys from Dad's hand. 'See that the bags get upstairs immediately,' she ordered. 'I'm going for a shower. Where's the nearest elevator?'

'I'm afraid there are no elevators,' said Dad. 'But your rooms are only on the first floor.'

'No elevators?' screeched Beachbabe. 'You mean I have to walk upstairs to get my shower?'

'Sorry, no showers either,' apologised Dad. 'Not enough water pressure, you see. But there's plenty of hot water, you can have a very nice bath.'

Beachbabe muttered something unprintable and teetered upstairs on her scarlet high heels.

Roderick James McCrumble, the third, gave Dad an embarrassed smile and muttered, 'Women.'

R.J. just pulled his baseball cap even lower over his eyes and scuffed his trainers on our threadbare rug.

Dad handed out the registration forms that always have to be filled in and the two men started into a deep conversation about their McCrumble ancestors. I was just taking R.J. to sample some of Kirsty's shortbread when there was an almighty yell.

'That's Beachbabe,' sighed Roderick McCrumble. 'I'd recognise that screech anywhere.'

'Oh dear,' said Dad. 'I wonder if Millie and Max are snoozing in the bath again. They tend to do that in warm weather.'

'I'll go and find out,' I volunteered.

'I'll come too,' said R.J.

We raced upstairs and found Beachbabe in the bathroom, standing on top of the loo seat. Millie and Max were between her and the door. Millie was looking at her quizzically, head on one side, while Max danced a doggy jig on the tiled floor. Here was someone new to play with. Perhaps standing on the toilet seat was a new game. He usually just drank the toilet water when no one was looking. Perhaps she did that too.

Beachbabe was stiff with fright. 'Get these creatures away from me,' she yelled.

'They're not *creatures*,' I protested. 'They're Millie and Max. They live here. They're family. They're also very friendly, they just want to play.'

'Well, I don't play with canines,' said Beachbabe. 'And I want another room. One with an en suite bathroom and no hairy mutts.'

'We don't have any en suite rooms,' I said. 'Dad would've made that clear when you booked. This is the only bathroom.'

'But it's miles away from my bedroom,' howled Beachbabe.

R.J. stuck his head out into the hallway. 'At least a metre and a half,' he grinned, 'and all downhill.'

'Subsidence,' I agreed. 'But it's always been like that. I used to like to ride my red tricycle down it when I was little.'

'Tell your father I want to speak to him immediately, R.J.,' said Beachbabe. 'I just don't BELIEVE what this place is like. There is no WAY I am staying here.'

But she was.

Roderick J. McCrumble, the third, wasn't the head of McCrumble Industrial Waste Products for nothing. He would have none of Beachbabe's nonsense. They stayed. We heard the row from downstairs. It could probably be heard on the other side of the country in Inverness, possibly even in Edinburgh.

'I've been doing some research into my ancestors,' Roderick told us later when he was outside of one of Kirsty's finest steak pies, 'and I'm determined to get as close to them as possible. There can be nowhere better than the Crumbling Arms, where the very walls are made from the old castle stones. Perhaps the spirit of my ancestors in those very walls will speak to me.'

As if on cue, there was a banging and a clanking and those very walls seemed to shiver and shake.

Roderick McCrumble's face paled, and his eyes grew large in his head.

'They're speaking to me,' he whispered.

'Well, I hope they're telling you to go home,' muttered Beachbabe, who'd refused Kirsty's steak pie in favour of a hamburger from the chippy.

'It's probably just the plumbing,' I whispered to R.J. as I cleared away his plate. He had enjoyed Kirsty's shortbread *and* the steak pie.

But he gave me a wink and said, 'I think you've come to the right place, Dad. I'm sure I can feel the old McCrumble vibes as well. I think we should stay as long as we can.'

Sneaky fellow. I decided there and then that I quite liked him, and gave him an extra large helping of Kirsty's world famous chocolate cake.

Chapter 7

When R.J. had finished his dinner I took him to meet Donk. We went out to the back yard through the kitchen and bumped into Kirsty carrying a tray full of dishes.

'Och, mind where you're going, Kat McCrumble,' she said. 'Have you not two eyes to see with?'

'Let me help you with that tray, ma'am,' said R.J., coming to the rescue. 'Would you like me to put it on the kitchen table?'

'Well, I'm glad to see someone in this place has manners.' Kirsty beamed at him.

I raised my eyes heavenwards. 'R.J., this is Kirsty, our cook. Kirsty, this is R.J.' See, I have manners too. But not as polished as some.

'Are you the Kirsty that made the chocolate cake?'

'I am.'

'It was the very best I have ever eaten, ma'am, and I have eaten a lot of chocolate cake in a lot of places.'

This boy wasn't real!

Kirsty's smile widened. 'Well that's very nice of you to say so, Archie.'

'Archie!' I giggled.

'Actually, I like that much better than R.J. or Roderick James. From now on I shall call myself Archie. Archie McCrumble. Thank you, Kirsty. I'm much obliged.'

I hauled him out of the kitchen before he could smarm any more, but not before Kirsty had given him a piece of her millionaire shortbread. Perhaps that boy knew a thing or two.

'Are you always so charming?' I asked on our way across the yard.

'Only to cooks,' he mumbled, his mouth full of chocolate caramel. I noticed he wasn't charming enough to offer me any. 'It's the first rule of survival when you're at boarding school. Get friendly with the cook. That way you eat better.'

'Boarding school?' I was intrigued. My school was only a bus ride away.

'Yep, it's easier than trying to live with Mom or

Dad.' And he changed the subject. 'Did you know that a male donkey is called a jackass and a female donkey a jenny?'

'Of course,' I said, feeding a carrot to Donk. I didn't, but I wasn't going to admit that to clever trousers, and I knew Donk wouldn't tell on me. 'Donk's a rescue donkey,' I went on. 'The SPCA rehomed him with us.'

'I wish someone would rescue me to a place like this,' sighed Archie.

'Why, you're not being ill treated, are you?'

'No,' said Archie, 'it's just . . . well, Beachbabe's not my mom, thank goodness. You probably realised that.'

'Uh-huh.'

'Mom's back home in the States. She's only on husband number four so Dad's one up on her at the moment.'

'Why do they marry so many people? Is it a competition?'

Archie shrugged. 'Who knows? I think they both still love each other, but won't admit it. They are so stubborn. When I'm staying with Mom she wants to know all about what Dad's been doing, and when I'm with Dad he wants to know all about Mom. I just wish they'd get together again, so we could go back to how it used to be. Then I wouldn't feel so much like a parcel being pushed between them.'

I said nothing, but gave him a carrot from the bag to feed Donk. He scratched Donk's odd-shaped nose and whispered, 'Hi there, old fellow. How're you doin'? Do you like that? There's nothing like a good scratch, is there?'

Donk gave an encouraging little rumble in his throat. He's usually very wary of strangers, but he obviously liked Archie. That was good enough for me.

'You can help me brush him tomorrow,' I offered, 'and help me feed the other animals too, if you like.'

'That would be good,' said Archie. 'I like animals. You love them, they love you back. They're less complicated than humans and much more reliable, and they don't play pass the parcel with you.'

There was no answer to that.

Chapter 8

Over breakfast next morning Roderick and Beachbabe had another of their loud arguments. I couldn't help overhearing. Neither could Lachy McCrumble out on his boat in the middle of Loch Bracken. The noise probably scared away the fish.

Beachbabe, dressed completely in banana yellow, including lipstick and feathery earrings, was not happy.

'When can we leave this awful place?' she demanded to know. 'I didn't sleep a wink last night.'

'Must have been someone else, then, who was snoring beside me,' muttered her husband.

'I do not snore. I have never been known to snore.' Beachbabe's tone was steely.

'Did you know that snoring is caused by the vibration of the soft palate if you breathe through your nose and mouth?' said Archie, to no one in particular.

'Shut up, R.J.,' said Beachbabe.

'There's no need to be rude,' said Roderick.

I hovered on the edge of the row with my note pad, waiting to take their breakfast order. At a slight pause in the hostilities, I cleared my throat. Very diplomatically, I thought.

'Good morning, everyone,' I said brightly. 'Are you ready to order breakfast?'

'Yes,' said Roderick, pleased by the interruption. 'I'll have some of your special creamy porridge.'

I made a note. 'Would you like a scattering of home-grown strawberries on top? Jinty McCrumble, who has the bakery, left two punnets on the doorstep early this morning, in exchange for some of Kirsty's rum truffles.'

'Lovely,' said Roderick.

'Make that two,' said Archie.

'I want a Hershey bar,' said Beachbabe.

'I'm sorry,' I said, 'but I don't think we have those.'

'Huh! If we were in a proper hotel I'd be able to order anything I liked. As it is, it looks like I'm going to be starved to death.'

'Well, if you won't eat proper food . . .' said Roderick.

'I'll eat what I want to eat. Don't you try to tell me what to do, you McCrumble you!'

Archie took out his book of 1001 interesting facts about seaweed and started to read it. I escaped to the kitchen and left Dad to attend to Beachbabe. Left to me, I'd have offered her lumpy custard to go with her banana yellow look.

Finally she settled on two eggs over easy. I cooked them really carefully and took them in to her.

'These yolks look very yellow,' she complained. 'Have you done something with them?'

'Just fried them,' I said.

'You haven't added yellow food colouring to them?'

'No, that's the colour they were when they came out of the hen's b—, out of the shell,' I said.

'Well, they don't look right. I'm sure they will raise my cholesterol level.'

Right now, she was raising my temper level.

'At least they match your outfit,' I said brightly, and hurried back to the kitchen.

Fortunately, the hire car Dad had organised for Roderick and Beachbabe arrived soon after, and, still sniping at each other, they departed for Inverness. Roderick was going to the library to do some further research into his family tree, while Beachbabe did the shops. The shops wouldn't know what had hit them. I hoped they stocked plenty of shorts.

When it was finally quiet, Archie came into the kitchen. 'Sorry about all that,' he muttered. 'They're always rowing. There'll be another divorce soon.' And he helped himself to the last of my toast. He'd already munched his way through the mountain I'd put on his breakfast table. That boy could eat for the USA.

'If you're quite finished,' I said pointedly, 'we can go and feed the animals.' I nearly said *other* animals, but that would have been rude, and, when you run an inn, you're not supposed to be rude, or lose your temper. So Dad says. I must try to remember.

We headed out to see Emily, the tarantula, first. Emily's human family had gone off to Spain on holiday which was why she was boarding with us. When I opened the door of her outhouse she was sitting quietly on top of a little tree in her vivarium.

'You don't have to worry about Emily,' I told Archie. 'She's quite tame and won't bite, unless she's provoked.'

Archie didn't seem a bit worried. 'I like spiders,' he said. 'Did you know that a true tarantula is really a wolf spider from southern Europe, and was named after the town of Taranto in Italy?'

This boy was a real anorak.

'And that in 1998 a Scottish spider breeder bred a goliath tarantula with a leg span of 280 millimetres?'

This anorak was beginning to annoy me. I gave Emily her food – a small dead mouse Dad had found on the doorstep earlier. We use road kill for Emily whenever possible, though I suspect Samantha may have been responsible for the mouse. The door of the outhouse creaked slightly as the lady herself slid in. She strolled by and gave us her superior look.

'That's Samantha,' I said.

'I know,' said Archie. 'I read her name on her collar when we met earlier on the stairs. She's a beauty.' And do you know, that fickle feline came and rubbed her head against Archie's leg and let him stroke her ears.

We had just finished feeding Charlie, the rabbit, and Nelson and Horatio, the guinea pigs, when Morag arrived with the post. As usual, Millie and Max bounded to greet her, and all five of us, plus Morag's postbag, struggled to get through the kitchen door at once. The dogs won.

Morag chatted over her cup of tea then grew very quiet as she handed over another long white envelope to Dad. I looked at her and she just shook her head. Even Archie had shut up for a moment about the many interesting things he knew about the Penny Black, though only after I had threatened to stamp on his head.

Dad opened the letter. 'It's from C.P. Associates,' he said unnecessarily. 'They have upped their offer for the inn, though not by much.'

'Is that it?' I asked.

'Not quite,' frowned Dad. 'Read that last sentence.'

I took the letter from him and read it. If steam really could come from your ears, I'd have had enough to power an old train on the West Highland line, for, after their second derisory offer for the inn, C.P. Associates had advised Dad that ... 'It would be in your best interests to accept our offer as no further offer will be made, and you may very well regret turning it down.'

Now what exactly did that mean? Was I wrong to detect a threat?

I looked at Morag. She looked grim. I didn't need the second sight to see that she was concerned too.

Later, I filled Archie in on all the details. After all, he was a McCrumble too, even if he was a knowledge nut.

'Was there a threat in that letter?' I asked. 'Or am I just being paranoid?'

Archie took off his baseball cap and scratched his head. 'I don't know,' he said. 'But my dad always says, just because you're paranoid doesn't mean they're not out to get you.'

He was such a comfort, that boy.

Chapter 9

To make matters worse, Ron Jackson was in the bar that evening.

I just don't trust that man. I don't know why. Perhaps it's some instinct left over from cave girl days where, if a smiling stranger arrived hiding two large clubs behind his back, you might think, 'Hey wait a minute, perhaps I shouldn't trust this guy.' I don't know.

Ron Jackson certainly smiled a lot. But it wasn't a genuine smile. There was something false about it, and about the way he slapped everyone on the back and bought them drinks. You can't buy friendship, not real friendship. He had tried to get friendly with Donald, perhaps because Donald knows a lot about the estate, but Donald would have none of it. Even when Ron Jackson offered him a full-time job on the estate, Donald was polite to him, but nothing more. And he certainly didn't respond to Ron Jackson's offer to look round the interesting trees. Donald already knows all the trees on the estate. Visits them most days and sits in some of them, but Ron Jackson never spots him.

Archie, I knew I could trust. I'd only known him for a couple of days, but apart from his tendency to show off his encyclopaedic knowledge about practically everything, he was OK. The animals thought so too, so I took Archie to my special corner. It's behind all the runs and pens in the back yard and just on the edge of the forest. I'd set up a little bird table there, and hung out nut feeders and red net nut bags. I scattered wild bird food every day too, including some of Kirsty's sunflower seeds when she wasn't looking. But it wasn't only the birds who came to the table.

Archie and I settled down behind a large hawthorn bush to watch. At first the bird table was empty, then, as the stillness settled down around us, there was a flash of colour, and a greater spotted woodpecker swooped down to feed. He was a glorious sight with his black and red head and his black and white spotted tail. But he had a problem. He was a little too big for the nut feeders and his beak was way too long. Undaunted, he gripped the bottom of a nut feeder, leaned out from it like a dinghy sailor, and made room for his beak. His rapid pecking demolished the peanuts in no time. Then he took off on a looping flight and disappeared into the trees.

We sat a bit longer till the blue tits and greenfinches arrived, closely followed by a whole host of chaffinches. And shortly afterwards a special visitor came. A red squirrel. Not a grey one, incomers from Canada and the States, but a beautiful chestnut-coloured squirrel with tufty ears and a bushy tail. The watery sunlight shone through his tail as he scampered across the little bit of open ground from the forest and leapt up on to the bird table. He hung on to a red nut bag and nibbled a hole in the bottom till . . . jackpot! All the peanuts fell out on to the ground. He followed them down and his feast began. Unfortunately, the rain began too, but he simply curled his bushy tail over his head and sat under his 'umbrella' till he'd finished his meal. After that, he buried some nuts in the grass for later and disappeared back into the forest.

I gave a happy sigh.

'Magic,' said Archie. 'Did you know that—'

'Yes,' I said. 'I know all about red squirrels being threatened with extinction because of the greys.'

Come to think of it, I was feeling a little bit threatened myself. By C.P. Associates. I tried to put the thought out of my head. I was getting to be as bad as Morag.

The rest of the day Archie and I spent out on the hills with Millie and Max, trying to spot golden eagles. We didn't see any, but we did see lots of buzzards and sparrow-hawks and kestrels. I think kestrels are amazing – they can drop from the sky like a stone when they spot their prey. The birds we saw were all hovering over the estate looking for food; their version of supermarket shopping.

Eventually we returned home, tired and hungry.

The inn was quiet. No sound of any rowing. We discovered that Roderick and Beachbabe had gone elsewhere for dinner.

'Probably to one of those fast-food places,' sniffed Kirsty. And, since there were no other guests, she gave Archie and me our dinner in the kitchen.

'This makes me feel more like family, Kirsty,' said Archie. 'I like it.'

Kirsty liked Archie. She liked the way he devoured her mince and tatties. 'My, you've a grand appetite for such a skinny laddie,' she said. 'You're a McCrumble and no mistake. But we'll have to feed you up and put some meat on your bones. There's no way you could hold up a kilt at the moment. It would fall about your feet.' And she piled his plate high with more food.

Archie grinned and tucked in. We were just polishing off large slices of apple tart when the cat flap slowly opened. I motioned Archie to be quiet and still as a black and white stripey head appeared and looked round. Seeing no immediate danger, the head was followed by a chubby black body. It was Flip.

Archie couldn't believe his eyes. I smiled at him and we both watched as Flip padded across the kitchen floor. His large claws made little clicking noises as he went. He stopped when he reached Samantha's dish. It was empty. I got up quietly and opened a tin of chicken liver cat food. Flip smelled it right away and snaffled it out of the dish as fast as I could spoon it in. Finally he licked the bowl clean. Then, well satisfied, he headed back the way he'd come in, squeezing his large rear through the cat flap and out into the night.

For once Archie was speechless.

'Well?' I grinned.

'You have a badger for a friend!' he exclaimed. 'A

wild animal! You are so lucky to live here with all this wildlife.'

'I know,' I grinned. I just loved Auchtertuie and the whole area round about. Not that I didn't want to visit other places. I did. But it's not easy to get away when you run an inn, and cash is always a bit tight.

But not everyone thought we were lucky to have the wildlife. When Archie and I slipped into the bar later to get a Coke, Ron Jackson was laying forth about how the wildlife was eating into his game stock. About how there wouldn't be as much for the hotel guests to shoot this year. About how difficult it made his job.

I paused with my Coke halfway to my lips. Now, I know I'm supposed to keep my temper. I know I'm not supposed to get cross with the customers. I know I'm supposed to keep my mouth firmly shut. And *you* know pigs might fly.

'The wildlife were on the estate before you were, Mr Jackson,' I said. 'And they like to eat too, just like you.'

One or two of the locals grinned. Ron Jackson's pot belly clearly showed he was no stranger to the table.

He saw people smiling and gave me a nasty look. 'I wasn't talking to you, miss,' he said. 'You shouldn't be in here where adults are. You should be in bed playing with your dolls or talking to your teddy bear.'

I opened my mouth to protest, but Dad gave me a warning look.

'Just take your drink and go, Kat,' he said quietly.

My face was the same colour as my hair, as Archie and I left the bar.

'What a horrible guy,' said Archie. 'Good thing he didn't know about Flip being in the kitchen. Probably would have shot him or at least had you closed down.'

'You'd never tell him,' I said, alarmed.

Archie gave me a withering look. 'Don't be three kinds of an idiot,' he said.

'OK,' I said and smiled.

Some people you just know you can trust.

Chapter 10

Beachbabe wasn't happy. She came thundering downstairs next morning and barged straight into the kitchen, where I was helping Dad prepare the breakfasts. She stood in front of us, hands on hips.

'Just look at my legs,' she stormed. 'Just look at them.'

Dad and I looked at each other, then at her legs. They were perfectly ordinary legs. Very tanned and a bit skinny perhaps, but with the usual number of shins, knees and calves. More importantly, they went all the way up to her bum, which today was encased in eye-watering lime-green shorts.

'Er, what about your legs?' Dad was nonplussed.

'They've been bitten,' she said. 'Our bed must

have fleas. This inn is not clean, and it's no wonder with all these smelly animals everywhere. I am going to report you to the health authorities, the tourist board, the police!'

'Oh, now wait a minute,' protested Dad.

'Hang on, Dad,' I said. 'Can I ask you, Mrs McCrumble, where you had dinner last night?'

'What's that got to do with it?' asked Beachbabe. 'If you must know, it was in a restaurant by the lochside, a few miles away.'

'And, since it was a fine night, did you sit outside?'

'Yes, but what difference does that make?'

'Quite a lot,' I said, as Dad nodded. 'The marks on your legs are midge bites. Scotland is famous for its midgies. They thrive best near water, and, when you sat outside for dinner in your shorts, they thought *their* dinner had arrived too.'

Beachbabe frowned.

'And the animals are not allowed in your bedrooms,' said Dad, 'which are kept locked at all times.'

Beachbabe opened her mouth.

'Has your husband got bites?' I asked.

'No,' she muttered grudgingly.

'You see, he was wearing long trousers. If there were fleas in your bed, you'd both have bites.'

'Well, you would say that, wouldn't you?' sniffed Beachbabe. And she left, banging the kitchen door behind her.

Dad blew out his cheeks. 'The retail therapy didn't work then.'

'Nope,' I said. 'She's still as mad as a bag of cats.'

Breakfast was a silent affair. Beachbabe's mouth was set in a discontented line and my offer of some calamine lotion for her midge bites fell on stony ground. Roderick looked glum as he ate his porridge and even Archie was quiet. The silence was so intense I could hear their toast crunch.

Archie escaped to the kitchen as soon as he could.

'Inverness was a disaster,' he announced, pinching my toast again. 'Apparently Beachbabe didn't see a thing that she liked because the shops were all terrible.'

'But she came back with loads of carrier bags,' I said.

'Yep,' said Archie, 'but that's Beachbabe. Back home she has a closet full of clothes and nothing to wear.'

'What's she doing now?' I asked. 'Is it safe to go into the dining room to clear away the plates?'

Archie nodded. 'Dad's walking to the corner shop for his paper, and Beachbabe's gone upstairs to change into jeans to hide the bites on her legs.'

For about two minutes peace reigned. Dad loaded the dishwasher while I went into the dining room to collect the last of the breakfast things. I had just piled the empty cups up on my tray when . . .

'Aaaaargh!' It could only be Beachbabe.

Dad and I and Archie went running.

Beachbabe was standing in the middle of her bedroom floor, pointing.

'Look! Look!' she cried. 'You said there were no fleas, but look.'

We followed the line of her finger to the pillow on the rumpled bed.

'That's not a flea,' I said. 'That's a little spider.'

'Then I've been bitten by a spider. Oh, I feel ill. Is there an antidote? I need to see a doctor.'

'It's just a garden spider,' I said. 'Perfectly harmless. Look.' I picked it up gently and put it outside on the window ledge.

'Did you know that there are over thirty-five thousand kinds of spiders,' said Archie, just to be helpful. 'And they shed their skin up to ten times as they grow.'

'I don't care if they shed their heads,' said Beachbabe. 'Just keep them away from me.'

'We'll give your room an extra clean today, Mrs McCrumble,' soothed Dad. 'And I'll have Donald check for any little cracks the spiders might be getting through, but we are out in the country and spiders are inevitable, I'm afraid.'

How could Dad be so reasonable? I wanted to tell Beachbabe to grow up and shut up.

'I hate the countryside,' said Beachbabe. 'It's so full of . . . THINGS. Just keep the countryside and all its inhabitants well away from me!'

And she turned her back on all of us.

We left. Hurriedly.

'She doesn't want to stay here,' Archie told me on the way downstairs. 'She wants to go and stay in that fancy hotel on the estate, and she's been looking for an excuse. She's been moaning on about it to Dad. But he's happy here. Like me, he feels at home. Says he really can feel the spirits of his ancestors.'

'Does he?' I said, and had a little debate with myself about whether or not to tell Archie about seeing the ghost of Old Hamish. I didn't want him to laugh.

Finally, I decided to risk it.

'Wow,' he said when I'd finished my story. 'You really saw a ghost. Fantastic!'

'I thought he seemed friendly and nice,' I said. 'I got the feeling he wanted to help.'

And, funnily enough, later on that night Old

Hamish did help. Sort of. In a kind of a way. I think.

It was a quiet night with a clear sky and a full moon. The only sounds were the lapping of the water at the loch's edge and the occasional hoot of a barn owl in the trees. Everyone in the Crumbling Arms was tucked up tight and sleeping peacefully till suddenly there was a yell. A yell that could only come from relatives of the Loch Ness monster having a rave-up – or Beachbabe. Bedroom doors flew open and everyone rushed to see what was wrong. Beachbabe was standing at the top of the stairs, trembling.

'I saw a . . . I couldn't sleep,' she whispered. 'My bites were itching so I went to the bathroom to get some water to bathe them, and I saw a . . .'

'What?' I asked.

'A g-g-g-ghost. Just h-h-here, at the top of the stairs. He appeared, then disappeared.'

'What did he look like?'

'I don't know. Oh . . . long grey hair, a kilt and a kind of tartan shawl thing over his shoulder.'

'Old Hamish,' I said matter-of-factly.

Dad shook his head in disbelief.

'Old Hamish,' breathed Roderick. 'You saw Old Hamish, Beachbabe. You lucky thing. You're not even a real McCrumble. I wish I'd seen him.'

'Is that all you can say?' yelped Beachbabe, recovering fast. 'I get the fright of my life and all you can say is you wish *you*'d seen the ghost. Well, I do too. You can keep this crumbling old place. I've had enough of it. First thing in the morning I'm going back to civilisation. I'm going to the hotel on the estate, and you can come with me or not, as you like.' And she flounced back to her bedroom.

Roderick didn't like, and next morning Beachbabe left with her luggage piled high in Ali McAlly's taxi.

Everyone breathed a sigh of relief, including Roderick.

'She'll be happier being soothed and pampered,' he said.

'Good riddance, I say,' said Archie.

Nobody disagreed.

Chapter 11

For a little while after that things settled down. In between looking after the guests, Dad carried on improving the runs and pens in the back yard, while Archie and I took care of the animals. We took Donk over to the little beach by the lochside, where he happily let some of the small children have a ride on his back. Millie and Max came too. They like nothing better than swimming in the loch. They doggy-paddled furiously to be first to rescue the ball we threw. Samantha sat up in a nearby rowan tree giving us her slit-eyed gaze. She was much too superior to join us on the beach, but she liked to keep an eye on what was going on.

Donald would be up a tree somewhere too,

probably on the estate. He knew the habits of most of the wildlife there and was practically on speaking terms with the roe deer.

Archie's dad was still happily researching his family tree and tramping the countryside where his ancestors had lived, and Auchtertuie was its usual summer self, selling local crafts and tartan knick-knacks to the tourists. The weather was fine, i.e. not raining, and Jinty McCrumble's bakery cum tea shop was full to overflowing with people enjoying the home baking. The tourists could eat it faster than Jinty and Kirsty could make it. Luigi McCrumble, at the chippy, was doing a roaring trade in fish suppers while Evie McCrumble, at the tiny post office, was practically sold out of postcards and ice cream. Archie and I bought the last of the Cornettos, as a treat for ourselves and the pets, before we went back to the inn. Only the tourists were surprised to see Donk and the dogs waiting for us outside the post office; the locals were used to it. Everyone stopped to chat to us and stroke the animals. Donk and the dogs loved it, and I was just thinking how nice people were, and perhaps how silly I'd been to worry about C.P. Associates and the stupid letters, when the problems really started . . .

They began that night in the bar with Ron Jackson.

I was in the bar, helping Dad wash up some glasses, when Ron Jackson started complaining.

'My beer's flat,' he shouted at Dad. 'What kind of a pub is this that can't keep good beer?'

'I'm sorry,' said Dad mildly. 'I'll get you another pint.'

'Our beer's fine,' said a couple of the locals.

'Mine too,' agreed a passing hitch-hiker.

But Ron Jackson wasn't satisfied. Part way down his second pint he complained that it was cloudy.

'You're obviously not looking after it properly,' he told Dad. 'I don't think you know anything about beer.'

'I know enough,' said Dad patiently. 'Perhaps you should try a different kind.' And to my annoyance he gave Ron Jackson another free pint.

That one seemed to go down well enough till he got to the bottom of the glass.

'Aargh!' He let out a yell and put his hand to his mouth. 'Mouse droppings!' And he opened his hand and showed them round. 'They must have been at the bottom of the glass. No wonder the beer tastes terrible.'

By this time my temper was getting near exploding point and even Dad was annoyed.

'I don't see how that could have happened,' he said. 'The glasses are stored upside down.' And he gestured to the shelves on the back wall of the bar, where the gleaming glasses could be clearly seen.

'You probably had the mouse poo in your hand,' I said, unable to keep quiet. 'Just to get another free pint.'

There was a murmur of agreement from the other customers. Ron Jackson glowered and banged his glass down on the table as Dad opened the till. He gave Ron Jackson his money back.

'If you don't like the beer perhaps you should go elsewhere for a drink,' he suggested.

'Oh, don't worry,' said Jackson. 'I will, and I won't be back till this place has been completely renovated and made into a fit place to drink.'

'Renovated'? I raised my eyebrows questioningly at Dad. We had no intention of renovating the Crumbling Arms. We couldn't afford it. So what exactly did Ron Jackson mean? I opened my mouth to ask him, but he had gone, slamming the front door behind him.

Millie came out from under the table where she always stayed when Ron Jackson was about and looked at me, her head on one side.

'I don't know what he meant, Millie,' I said. 'I really don't know.'

But I didn't like it. Ron Jackson was bad news.

Chapter 12

Next day we had a power cut. Now, in Auchtertuie, that's not unusual. We sometimes get power cuts in wintertime when it's stormy and the power lines are blown down. When that happens, the whole village is in darkness, and there's nothing else to do but go to bed early. But this was summertime, the weather was fine, and we were the only ones affected. Everyone else had electricity.

We apologised to the people who had booked in for dinner, and Kirsty offered to make them ham salads. But it wasn't the same. They really wanted hot food, so we lost the business when most of them went elsewhere.

We had to apologise to the overnight guests as

well, as we hastily boiled pans of water on our two little emergency gas rings for their tea and coffee, and fed them cereal and fruit for breakfast. Porridge, bacon and eggs just weren't possible. I lit a fire in the lounge and Archie made toast using the old long-handled toasting fork that hung on the stone chimney breast. It was slow work, though Archie said the toast tasted great, and made some extra for himself later on.

The guests, three Swiss hillwalkers, were very understanding, and I made them up extra sandwiches in their packed lunches before they set off up Ben Bracken. I had just waved them goodbye when the van from the electricity supply company drew up and a spotty youth got out.

'Hi, Billy,' I said.

'Greetings, small McCrumble of the red thatch,' he said, in what he obviously imagined was an alien's voice. 'You sent for Billy, the Mighty Giver of Power. I am he and I am here.'

I grinned. Bampot Billy we called him behind his back and sometimes to his face. He was the older brother of Tina Morrison, my best friend.

'You'll find Dad in the kitchen,' I told him.

Billy went into the kitchen closely followed by Millie and Max. Dad was on his hands and knees inside a large cupboard looking for an ancient

Primus stove he knew we had somewhere.

'No need for that, Mr McCrumble,' Billy assured him. 'I'll find out what the problem is. People don't call me Billy the Brilliant for nothing.'

People didn't call him Billy the Brilliant at all.

But Max was impressed. While Millie sat and watched what was going on, he poked his nose in everywhere Billy did.

'Do you see this here, Max?' Billy was chatty. 'This is a power cable. We call it that because it's a cable with power running through it. Or not, as in this case. Got that?'

Max tried to look intelligent and failed.

'Now, Max,' Billy explained, 'we have to go and find out where the break in the power cable is. Come with me, O Hairy Helper, to the great outdoors, for there, I think, may lie the source of the problem.'

Again Max tried to look intelligent. Again he failed.

'Back yard, Max,' I said.

Max wagged his tail. He knew where the back yard was. He and Billy disappeared outside while Dad and I did the washing-up. The dishwasher sat silent and useless in the corner.

'Any luck?' asked Archie, returning from the corner shop with his dad's paper under his arm and a lollipop in his mouth.

'Not yet,' I said and handed him a tea towel. Archie looked mutinous.

'You're family,' I said. 'Family help dry the dishes. Get on with it.'

He muttered something unintelligible and picked up a plate. We were just down to the last of the cutlery when Billy returned.

'Did you manage to locate the break?' asked Dad.

'But of course,' said Billy, and flicked the light switch. 'Behold, power restored by Billy the Mighty, alias Billy the Brilliant.'

'Also known as Billy the Bampot,' I said to Archie.

'But only to those who do not understand my greatness,' nodded Billy.

'Great to have the power back on, Billy,' smiled Dad. 'What was the problem? Mice gnawing through the cable?'

Billy's spotty forehead wrinkled in a frown.

'No,' he said, in his normal voice. 'There was no evidence of teeth marks. It looked as though your power line had been deliberately cut. Now why would anyone want to do a thing like that?'

Billy left shaking his shaggy head. The rest of us were just standing there looking at each other when Kirsty arrived with a bag of fresh rolls for the lunchtime bar snacks. Morag followed her in with the mail. Hard on her heels was Roderick, to find out what had happened to his morning paper.

'What's wrong?' asked Morag, reading our expressions.

'You've faces like a tub of wet washing,' said Kirsty.

'Let's go, Archie,' said Roderick. 'These folks have matters to discuss, we don't want to intrude.'

'No, no,' said Dad. 'Stay. You may as well know. Someone deliberately cut our electricity cable.'

'Ron Jackson,' said Archie and I together.

'We don't know that,' said Dad. 'We've no proof.'

'But he's mean and horrible and the dogs don't like him,' I said.

'I doubt if that would stand up in court,' said Dad.

I had a sudden vision of Millie and Max in the witness box, holding their little right paws in the air and swearing to bark the truth, the whole truth and nothing but the truth.

'There's trouble ahead, Hector,' shivered Morag. 'I can feel its clammy presence creeping over me.'

'Probably that damp post office anorak,' said Kirsty. 'Sit down, all of you. We have electricity now so I'll make us all a cup of tea and a buttered scone. Then we can decide what to do. You should never make important decisions on an empty stomach.'

I smiled. Good old Kirsty. She thought there was nothing that couldn't be fixed with a cup of tea and a bit of home baking.

We talked round the problem for a while then decided to do nothing, apart from tell Constable Ross what had happened. What else could we do? We had no proof.

'We'll just have to be vigilant,' said Dad, 'and keep a lookout for any trouble.'

Easier said than done.

Chapter 13

To make matters worse, Donald came into the kitchen later that morning looking grim.

'Whatever's the matter, Donald?' said Kirsty, abandoning the rolls we were buttering for lunch. 'Come and sit down, you're as white as your frock.'

'The badger baiters are definitely here,' he said, slumping into a chair. 'I've just seen the evidence. I was over on the estate, doing my usual tree rounds, when I came across the remains of a male badger outside his sett.'

'It wasn't—' I gasped.

'No, it wasn't Flip,' he said. 'The sett was on the far side of the estate. I've reported the whole matter to Constable Ross.'

'He's having a busy day,' I said, and told Donald about our problem.

'Och, it never rains but it pours,' said Kirsty, and poured Donald out some tea.

Archie and I left them to it and took Millie and Max out for a walk.

'And to think I thought Auchtertuie would be a quiet little place where nothing much ever happened,' said Archie, looking over his shoulder at the row of tidy little shops and houses that hugged the edge of the loch. 'How wrong could I be? There's some lunatic cutting electricity cables and other lunatics badger baiting. What next?'

'That's the trouble,' I said, throwing a ball for Millie and Max. 'There's too much happening at the moment for Constable Ross to cope with. He can't be everywhere, and there are so many badger setts, the badger baiters could be anywhere at any time.'

'So what can we do?' asked Archie. 'We have to be alert for dirty tricks at the Crumbling Arms. *We* can't be in two places at once either.'

'Not during the day,' I said thoughtfully. 'But the badger baiters operate at night, deep in the forest. How brave do you feel . . . ?'

We decided not to tell the grown-ups that we were going to look for the badger baiters. They would only worry, and Dad had enough on his mind fretting about the Crumbling Arms. Roderick had offered to help Dad keep a lookout. The Crumbling Arms was his ancestral home too.

After lunch, Archie and I spent some time in my room, making plans. I drew up a rough map of the estate and pinpointed some badger setts.

'These are just the ones I know about,' I said. 'But there will be others.'

'There are so many.' Archie shook his head. 'How will we know where to look?'

'We won't. But that's no excuse for not trying.'

'You sound like my third grade teacher,' Archie grinned. 'What shall we take to eat?'

That boy was all mouth and stomach.

'A flask of Kirsty's soup,' I said.

'Tomato's my favourite.'

'OK.'

'Actually, two flasks would be better. We must keep our strength up. We don't want to get frostbite.'

'This is Scotland in summer,' I retorted. 'Not the Arctic circle.'

At that moment, despite the watery sun, a little flurry of hail hit my bedroom window.

'OK,' I agreed, 'two flasks.'

Later that night, after Kirsty had gone home, I

sneaked a box of her tomato soup from the freezer, warmed it up, and put it into flasks. Then I went to bed as normal and waited till everyone was asleep. I lay under my duvet fully clothed except for my boots. When I thought it was safe, I tiptoed along the corridor and, as arranged, tapped three times on Archie's door. He opened it straight away and the two of us crept downstairs to the kitchen. Millie and Max were immediately awake, tails wagging.

'Perhaps we should take them,' suggested Archie.

I shook my head. 'Millie would be fine, Max would give us away.' Anyway, I had already thought about it and had two doggy chews in my anorak pocket to keep them happy and quiet.

We slipped out. Dad had double-locked the kitchen door and I had to remember to take the key and relock it behind me. We crept out across the back yard, past the runs and pens, past a sleeping Donk, and headed for the little clearing where I'd set up the bird table. It was empty, though I saw two eyes blink at us from the nearby trees. Archie started.

'Only a fox,' I said. 'He won't bother us.'

The night was cool and, being the north of Scotland in summertime, not properly dark. But, when we slipped into the forest, we needed our torches.

'Save the battery in yours for coming back,' I whispered to Archie. 'We'll just use mine.'

We trudged along for ages, dodging tree roots and overhanging branches. I stopped every so often to check my little silver compass. Though my instinct told me we were headed in the right direction, the forest can be deceiving in the dark. We tried to be as quiet as possible, but heard scurrying in the undergrowth as mice, foxes and deer kept well away from us. Only the owls protested at our presence and we both nearly jumped out of our socks when one flew so close we could hear the whirr of its wings.

We were headed for a badger sett that I thought could be a likely target. It was deep enough into the forest to give the badger baiters cover, but not too deep to give them transport problems.

The night had grown darker now and the pale moon couldn't quite penetrate the canopy of trees. I could hear Archie breathing hard behind me.

'We're almost there,' I whispered, then motioned him to be still.

I switched off the torch and we both stood and listened. It was eerily quiet. No scufflings. No scurryings. Not even a protesting owl. I listened more intently. There was a faint sighing as a light breeze stirred the trees. After a few moments, I thought I could detect a rustle in the undergrowth, possibly some badgers playing outside their sett. The ground was damp beneath my feet and I could feel rain in the air. I could also feel something else. Something indefinable. My senses were tingling. Maybe I was getting to be as bad as Morag, but I was sure I could feel . . . a presence.

This is crazy, I thought. You're letting your imagination run away with you, Kat McCrumble. And I gave myself a shake.

'Come on, Archie,' I whispered and switched on my torch again.

That's when the 'presence' landed on us and sent us crashing to the ground.

I yelled. Archie yelled. The 'presence' yelled.

I recognised that yell. That was no 'presence'. That was . . . 'Donald!' I gasped.

'Kat!' gasped Donald.

'There's an elbow in my ear,' gasped Archie.

Shakily, the three of us stood up. Archie felt around for the torch he had dropped and switched it on. Mine had gone out.

Donald was angrier than I've ever seen him.

'What are you two doing out here at this time of night?' he demanded. 'You should be at home. Do your fathers know about this?'

I deliberately ignored that last bit. 'I expect we're

80

doing the same as you, Donald, looking for the badger baiters. I thought this might be a likely spot for them.'

'Me too,' said Donald. 'I thought that's who you were.'

'But you shouldn't have tried to tackle them on your own,' I said.

'And you shouldn't be out here without your dad knowing,' said Donald.

'But Dad wouldn't have let us come if he'd known.'

'I should think not.' Donald was calmer now. 'I should tell him. Suppose something had happened to you?'

I thought for a moment. 'Dad might not think it so bad if we were out here with a responsible adult . . . That's you,' I added, in case Donald didn't recognise the description. 'And if we had our mobiles with us . . .'

Donald looked blank, and I remembered he'd never used a mobile phone in his life. Probably no pockets in his frock.

'I'll give you my old mobile and show you how to use it,' I offered. 'That way we can phone for help if necessary.'

Even by torchlight, the indecision on Donald's face was plain. This was not the kind of decision your average druid usually had to make.

'Constable Ross can't possibly do this on his own,' I added. 'He doesn't know the woods as well as we do. And who else is there to help the badgers?'

That settled it.

'OK,' said Donald, 'but only if you promise to be really careful.'

'We will, won't we, Archie?'

'You bet,' said Archie. 'Now, if there really are no bad guys round here, do you think we could have our soup? Being flattened by a druid always makes me peckish.'

Chapter 14

We slipped back into the inn, undetected. Millie and Max half opened an eye, half wagged a tail and went back to sleep. Samantha, however, who slid in through the cat flap while we were tiptoeing through the kitchen, gave us her 'And what precisely are you doing here at this time of night?' look.

I gave her my 'Ask no questions and you'll be told no lies' look, so she just flicked her ears and yawned.

'I'm really glad cats can't clype,' I whispered to Archie.

'Clype?'

'Tell tales.'

'Uh-huh,' he said softly and padded off to his room.

I headed upstairs too, undressed and got into bed. Despite the night's excitement, I fell asleep immediately, but not for long enough. When my alarm went off at 6.45 a.m., I had to drag myself out of bed. I threw on my clothes, deciding to wash later, and ran downstairs to help with the breakfasts.

'What's up, Kat?' said Dad, just back from his morning swim in the loch. 'You look like you've hardly slept.'

'I didn't get much sleep last night,' I said, truthfully. I didn't want to tell Dad what we'd been up to, but I didn't want to lie to him either.

Archie and Roderick hadn't yet appeared so we only had two guests for breakfast. They were a Belgian husband and wife who had come over on the ferry from Zeebrugge to Rosyth and were touring the Highlands in their caravan.

'We will have the full Scottish breakfast,' they beamed at me as I took their order. 'We like so much the black pudding and the fried tattie scones.'

I smiled and hoped I could keep my eyes open long enough to cook them.

While the bacon and black pudding were grilling, I turned on the tap to fill the kettle for tea. There was a groaning sound and the water came through noisy and sputtering.

'Probably some air in the pipes,' said Dad. 'Turn the tap on a bit more to see if it clears.'

It didn't. Instead the water turned bright red. I clutched Dad's arm.

'There's blood in the pipes,' I moaned.

'What on earth!' said Dad. 'Of course it's not blood. It can't be . . . look, run along to Jinty's and see if her tap water's the same colour. If it's not, get some water for the guests' tea while I investigate.'

I hurried along to the bakery with dread in my heart. Dad said it wasn't blood coming out of the tap but it looked very like it to me. A little shakily I told Jinty what had happened.

'Let me check, Kat,' she said, and turned on the tap in the little sink at the back of the shop. The water ran clear.

'It's just us, then,' I said, as she handed me a kettle full of clean sweet water.

I ran back to the inn. Dad was looking worried. 'The water's the same in the bathroom upstairs,' he said. 'We sometimes get brackish water after there's been a storm, but never that colour.'

'And last night was fine,' I said. 'A little bit of rain, but not much.'

Dad looked at me.

'We would have heard a storm,' I added hastily.

'I must go and check the water tank in the attic,' he said, 'and see if there's anything I can do till the plumber gets here.'

I had just finished serving the breakfasts when Archie and Roderick appeared in the kitchen, still in their bathrobes. Their faces and hands were very pink. So was their hair.

'The water seems to have turned us a funny colour,' said Roderick. 'Is this an old Scottish custom? I haven't read about it in any of the history books.'

'No,' said Dad, coming into the kitchen, grim-faced. 'The attic window has been prised open and I found these beside the water tank.' He held out several small bottles of red food colouring. 'If this is someone's idea of a joke, it's not very funny.'

Dad turned on all the taps to run away the red water and eventually the water ran clear. Roderick and Archie went to wash away the pinkness. We were lucky they were the only ones affected. Other guests could have complained and had us closed down. Things were getting worse, and the last line of the letter from C.P. Associates came into my head . . .

'It would be in your best interests to accept our

offer as no further offer will be made, and you may very well regret turning it down.'

But, while the red water incident had been a bit scary, it was nothing compared with what happened next.

Chapter 15

All of a sudden our local supplies of meat and fish dried up.

'I'm really sorry, Hector.' James Ross, the butcher, was apologetic on the phone to Dad. 'But the big hotel on the estate has decided to take practically everything I've got. They're paying extra for it, on the understanding that I don't supply anyone else. I just can't afford to turn down the business.'

Dad was annoyed, but resigned. I was madder than a bee in a bottle.

Before Dad could stop me, I stormed out of the inn and along the road to the butcher's shop. It was still early and James Ross was filling up his refrigerated counter display. Coils of plump sausages sat piled in a corner beside his tasty mealy puddings. He was just leaning into the display to put the price ticket on his best lean mince when I yelled at him.

'Just what do you think you're doing, cutting off our supplies!'

James Ross's head, in its white butcher's hat, came up so fast it cracked itself on the inside of the glass counter. 'Whaaaat?'

He reached out to steady himself and plunged one hand into his best lean mince and the other into the pile of plump sausages, some of which burst under his weight and slithered to the floor.

It was his turn to yell. 'Kat McCrumble! Just what do you think YOU'RE doing?'

'What I'M doing?' I yelled back. 'I'm not the traitor. I'm not the snake in the grass. I'm not the one who turns his back on his friends whenever it suits him.'

'I'm not turning my back,' said James Ross. 'I—'

'You should be ashamed of yourself,' I said and swept out. 'Don't buy the mince or the sausages,' I advised incoming customers. 'There's been a snake on them.'

When Kirsty heard about the problem with the meat supplies, she stormed along too. But the outcome was the same.

'James Ross says he needs the extra business to carry him through the winter when the tourists have gone and trade is slack,' she reported.

'That's no excuse,' I muttered. 'Business is slow for everyone in winter.'

It was the same story with the fish suppliers. The 'big' hotel was offering prices we couldn't possibly match. Only Lachy McCrumble out on his fishing boat in the middle of the loch promised to give us everything he caught. Unfortunately, Lachy never caught much more than a cold.

'I'll just have to go to the cash and carry in Inverness two or three times a week to get supplies,' said Dad.

'But it won't be the same, Hector,' said Kirsty. 'People come here to eat because they know we use James Ross's beef, which is the best for miles around. And they know that I choose it and cook it myself.'

'I realise that,' sighed Dad. 'But there's no point in crying over spilt milk or lost beef, and it's the best I can do at the moment.'

That night, for the first time ever, when folks appeared for dinner, we had to turn them away. We just didn't have enough food to give them. Kirsty got really angry and upset, so upset that a whole pot of tea wasn't enough to calm her down. She decided she needed stronger medicine. She went to the dresser, to the blue and white jar marked 'Flour', took out the bottle of malt whisky, and poured herself a large glass. At first she sipped it quietly, then the whisky took effect.

'Step we gaily, on we go . . .'

The customers in the bar winced when they heard Kirsty's attempt at 'Mhairi's Wedding', but they carried on chatting, just a bit louder. They couldn't do that though when she started playing the bagpipes. They wilted visibly when 'Flower of Scotland' drowned out their conversations. It sounded like half a dozen cats with their tails tied together, and I reckoned Kirsty could give up any hopes she'd ever had of joining the Auchtertuie Pipe Band. The customers downed their drinks and left. Quickly. Even Roderick and Archie, who loved all things Scottish, stuck cotton wool in their ears and decided to go to bed early with a good book.

Dad looked really worried as he closed the front door that night.

'We can't go on like this, Kat,' he said, 'or we'll be out of business in no time.' Then he saw my worried expression. 'But don't fret, I'll think of something. You go up to bed and I'll see that Kirsty gets home safely.'

Not long after, I heard Dad and Kirsty go out the back door.

'Shpeed bonnie boat like a birrrd on the wing.' Kirsty was attempting 'The Skye Boat Song' now.

'Shush, Kirsty,' said Dad. 'People are trying to sleep.'

'Shleep?' said Kirsty. 'Who wants to shleep? I want to party. Hic. Sorry. Pardon.'

'Poor Kirsty. Poor Dad,' I muttered, as I headed to the bathroom to clean my teeth. I pulled my dressing gown tighter round me at the sudden cold draught from the stairs. The front door must be open, I thought. Then I remembered I had seen Dad lock it. I looked up.

There, at the top of the stairs, was Old Hamish. I wasn't afraid. The feeling around him was benign.

'Hamish,' I whispered. 'I'm sure you know what's going on. What are we going to do? We can't sell the inn. We don't want to leave here. You don't want to be with strangers.'

Hamish shook his head and pointed to a picture on the wall. It was a computer generated image of how the original McCrumble castle might have looked. Dad had made it up after one of his researches into the family history. Puzzled, I looked back at Old Hamish. He balled his hand into a fist and shook it. Then, from his side he drew out an imaginary sword and waved it in the air. What was he trying to tell me?

Inspiration!

'We must fight to keep the inn. We must fight to save McCrumble castle! Is that what you mean, Hamish?'

Old Hamish nodded and faded away.

'Right,' I said pushing up the sleeves of my dressing gown and placing my hands on my hips. 'We'll do that. Oh yes, we'll do that.' And I was so fired up by my encounter with Old Hamish that I completely forgot what I was doing and cleaned my teeth twice.

It was only later on, in bed with my very clean teeth, that I started to wonder how on earth we were going to do it, and I went to sleep muttering, 'Save McCrumble castle'.

Chapter 16

In the middle of all this there were still the animals to look after. At least that side of the business was going well; the runs and pens at the back of the inn were full. Donk had a donkey friend called Lily, who had come to stay while her owners were on holiday. Donk liked Lily and Lily liked Donk. They nuzzled each other and played chases round and round their field. Donk was always sad when Lily went home. I fed him extra carrots when that happened and chatted to him for longer. We wanted to find another donkey as a friend for Donk, but couldn't afford it.

We had several more dogs to look after too, as well as Millie and Max. Some of the dogs were easier than others. We had two springer spaniels named Brandy and Ginger who were great escape artists, and we had to keep a close eye on them or they'd end up in Inverness. And there was Seamus, the largest, gentlest, Irish wolfhound in the world. He was such a gentleman and so polite. Too polite. When I fed the other dogs in the evening, he didn't join in the usual scrum, but stood back politely till the others had finished. Of course, they finished his dinner too, and he was left looking forlornly at an empty dish. I fed him separately once I realised. Some dogs are just too nice for their own good.

Samantha continued to provide us with food for Emily, who was quite happy to run up and down my arm for a bit of exercise.

'Most girls I know wouldn't play with spiders,' said Archie when he saw this. 'They'd scream and run away just at the thought.'

'Wimps,' I said. 'Anyway, if I'm going to be a vet when I grow up, I can't afford to be afraid of spiders.'

'Suppose not,' said Archie. 'That's what I like about you. You're quite fierce. You're not really like a girl. You're more like a . . . like a friend.'

'Hmm,' I muttered. I wasn't really sure of that 'not like a girl' bit. 'Do you know a lot of girls?'

'Some,' said Archie. 'Some are not real girls, they're like . . . relatives. Cousins and stuff.'

'What about girlfriends?' I asked, suddenly curious.

Archie blushed. 'Oh, loads of those, naturally.'

Yeah, right.

'What about you? What about boyfriends?'

It was my turn to blush. 'Oh, loads of those, naturally.'

OK, so we both lied. I have friends who are boys, but they're more into football and computers than anything else. Anyway, they say I'm bossy and quick-tempered and that's not true. Well, it's only a little bit true. I do have a bit of a temper sometimes, but only when I see things that are wrong. And bossy? *Moi?* Never.

Archie grinned at me. 'It's good to have a friend who's a girl,' he said. 'And it's really good to be here. This is my best holiday ever. I wish it could go on and on. I told Mom that when she phoned me last night.'

'Did you tell her about Beachbabe?'

'Yep, and she's delighted. I don't think things are too good between her and Edgar. That's husband number four. I think she might be about to give him the big elbow as well.'

I shook my head. 'You live in a different world,

Archie. It sounds strange, but fascinating. I don't know if my dad will ever marry again. Morag would like him to. Sends him a Valentine every year and signs it from "Guess who?" '

'Does he know it's from her?'

I shrugged. 'He just laughs and says it's from his secret admirer. Poor Morag, I don't know if Dad will ever notice her.'

'My dad's not taking any notice of Beachbabe. She's been phoning him constantly, demanding he join her in the big hotel. But he won't. He's happy here, same as me.'

I smiled. It was the longest conversation I'd had with Archie without him telling me a list of 'interesting facts' about something or other.

'Talking about Valentines,' said Archie. 'Did you know that St Valentine—'

I threw a handful of dried dog food at him.

'Shut up, Archie,' I said.

You can say that to boys who are friends.

Chapter 17

As if we didn't have enough problems, next day Beachbabe turned up at the inn. I had just finished clearing away the breakfast dishes, and was resetting the tables, when a white stretch limo slid past the dining-room window and stopped at the front door. A smartly dressed chauffeur sprang out and opened the passenger door. Beachbabe stepped out, not in shorts this time, but in a white miniskirt with gold and white fringes. She looked like the lampshade we have in the lounge. A gold and white fringed bra top and gold strappy sandals made sure she was matching. She obviously still liked to show off her tan, though with all the rain we'd had recently, it could possibly now be rust.

'Wait here,' she instructed the chauffeur.

He touched his cap and she strode to the front door of the inn. At least, it started off as a stride, but the strap on her left sandal broke, and she lurched forward in a kind of limping run. She threw out her arms to steady herself on the front door, just as I opened it. She fell into the hall. It wasn't a very graceful, ladylike fall, more of a bang and a clatter really.

'You did that on purpose,' she yelled at me.

'No, I didn't. You tripped over in those stupid shoes.' I reckoned I could say what I liked now that she wasn't a guest at the inn any more.

She glared at me and tried to regain her dignity. Not easy when you're on all fours. Millie and Max were pleased to see her though. Here was that funny lady who stood up on the toilet seat, come back to play another game. She was playing at being a dog this time, or was it a sheep? Millie licked Beachbabe's make-up off while Max tried to herd her into a corner.

'Get them off me!' screamed Beachbabe.

'Here, Millie. Here, Max,' I grinned.

Millie came smartly to heel. Max thought about it and decided 'Nah'. Instead he picked up the gold sandal by the broken strap and settled down to give it a good chew. It obviously tasted better than his normal doggy ones.

'Let go, Max,' I said, trying to wrest it from him.

Tug of war, thought Max. My favourite. Good game. Good game.

We danced back and forward across the hall, and by the time I had won the game, the sandal strap was well and truly slimy.

'Sorry,' I said, handing it to Beachbabe. 'Max likes to play.'

Beachbabe took the battered sandal and shuddered. 'Have you any idea how much these shoes cost?' she said.

'Nope,' I said cheerfully. 'Good thing the strap was broken before Max rescued it.' Replacing those shoes would have cost Dad a fortune.

The remnants of Beachbabe's gold eye-shadow glittered as she looked at me.

'Little Miss Clever Clogs, aren't we?' she said. 'But that won't last. Not once you and all your dumb animals are out of this place. Once you're closed down and out on the sidewalk, you won't be such a smart mouth then.'

'What do you mean?' I asked, my stomach doing backward rolls.

'Oh, I think you know. Once this place is taken over by C.P. Associates and made into a proper heritage site, tarted up into a tartan museum, with decent facilities, it'll start to make money. You should have sold it when you had the chance. As it is . . .' She let the words hang in the air. 'Now, where is my husband? Go and tell him I want to see him right now.' And she stamped her shoeless foot and nearly fell over again.

I'm not sure what I replied, but it must have been something about Roderick and Archie going out on Lachy McCrumble's boat to catch some fish for dinner. Anyway, Beachbabe turned on her one remaining sandal and left. She limped out to the limo as imperiously as she could and fell into the back seat. 'Tell my husband I'll be back,' she snarled and was gone.

I don't know how long I stood there, trying to make some sense of what I'd just heard. Millie and Max hovered round me, concerned. They knew something was wrong. Even Samantha, who had arched herself into the hall, came forward and rubbed her head against my leg. I must have looked really shaken.

'I must find Dad,' I said to them. 'I have to tell him about this. Things are even worse than we thought.'

Chapter 18

That evening, after a dinner of delicious sea trout caught by Archie, who was now insufferable, Dad called a family meeting. It was held in the kitchen round the big pine table. Kirsty had scrubbed it almost white over the years, but you could still make out KAT in faint red letters where I'd written my name in felt-tip pen when I was little. I was down by my name and looked round the table. Dad had asked Kirsty, Donald and Morag to attend as well as Roderick, Archie and Jinty. All the McCrumbles connected to the inn were present. The only non-McCrumble was Constable Ross.

'Right,' said Dad, when Kirsty had supplied everyone with a mug of tea and a slice of her best fruit loaf. 'I've asked you here because we have a problem.' And he told them all the things that had happened, starting with the letters from C.P. Associates, the severed electricity cable, the red water, and the problem with the local food supplies. Constable Ross blushed and shuffled at this point, since James Ross, the butcher, was his dad. My dad finished with my encounter with Beachbabe that morning.

'I'm sorry to have to tell you about Beachbabe,' Dad apologised to Roderick, 'but obviously she's heard something up at the estate.'

Roderick's face was grim. 'Don't give it another thought,' he said. 'She's only trying to get at me through you. I'm the one who should be apologising.'

'Actually, Beachbabe did us a favour,' I said. 'Now we know what this is all about. Now we know why C.P. Associates are trying to force us out of business.'

'But not what we can do about it,' said Constable Ross. 'Unfortunately, we have no proof of anything. Whoever has been up to these tricks has been careful to leave no clues, and your food supply drying up could be looked on as just sharp business practice, or even as the big hotel supporting the local community.'

'There is something else I think you should all know about,' said Donald. 'There's further evidence of badger baiting on the estate.'

'Where?' I asked.

'Near Millar's pond.'

'But that's not far from where we were looking the other ni—' I stopped, my face flaming. That always gave me away!

'You were out looking for badger baiters, Katriona?' frowned Dad. He only ever calls me Katriona when he's really annoyed. When I'm in real trouble.

'Sort of . . .' I muttered.

'Yes or no?' said Dad.

'Kind of . . .'

'Have you any idea how dangerous that is? What time of night were you out?'

'Latish.'

'I was there too,' volunteered Archie. Good lad, he wasn't letting me take the blame on my own.

'When was this?' It was Roderick's turn to be annoyed.

'Couple of nights ago,' Archie and I mumbled.

'But we didn't find them,' I said.

'No,' said Donald. 'I found Kat and Archie instead. I was out looking too.'

'You found this pair out in the woods and you

didn't tell me?' Dad's voice was incredulous. 'What kind of irresponsible behaviour is that?'

Everyone stared at the old table as though it had suddenly become really interesting. Dad was as mild as milk most of the time, till he got really cross, then the McCrumble temper, which he kept in check, started to show.

'It wasn't Donald's fault,' I protested. 'I asked him, pleaded with him, not to tell you. You had so much to worry about with all the things going wrong here. I knew Constable Ross couldn't be everywhere, and I know the estate nearly as well as Donald, and I just thought . . .'

'No, you didn't, Katriona,' said Dad. 'If you had stopped to think, you would not have put Archie's life in danger as well as your own. Do you think for one moment that people who consider it a sport to pit terriers against badgers, and who place bets on the outcome, would think twice about threatening you two? If not something worse?'

I gulped and stared into my mug. Archie played with the fruit loaf crumbs on his plate. Donald looked grim.

'We only wanted to help,' I muttered. 'And Donald made us promise only to go out again with him. We just can't let them get away with it, Dad. Suppose they get round to Flip's sett . . .'

The words were hardly out of my mouth when the cat flap slowly opened and a black head with a white stripe poked through. Flip looked around and gave a sniff. He knew there were more people around than normal. Everyone sat very still, except for me. I got up and moved slowly towards the badger. I pushed Samantha's dish with the chicken liver cat food in it towards him.

'There you go, Flip, old fellow. Dinner time.'

Flip gave the air another sniff, decided that we were all friendly, and lowered his head to eat. When the dish was clean, he turned tail and left the way he had come.

Everyone breathed out.

'You've a grand way with that badger, Kat McCrumble,' smiled Kirsty. 'You'll make a good vet one day.'

'That was awesome,' said Archie.

'Truly amazing,' agreed Roderick.

'You see.' I pressed home the advantage Flip's visit had given me. 'We can't sit back and do nothing. We can't let the badger baiters or C.P. Associates win. We must stand up for ourselves. We have to stand up for what's right.'

'Hear, hear,' said Morag. 'I'm with you, Kat.'

'And me,' said Archie.

'And me,' said Roderick.

'Count us in,' said Donald and Kirsty.

'You're a real McCrumble right enough, Kat,' said Jinty. 'What's the plan?'

'Now wait,' said Constable Ross. 'I agree with you, but you can't go taking the law into your own hands. I'm the law around here. I'll deal with any wrongdoers.'

'Fine, Constable Ross,' I said. 'But you'll have to catch them first.'

I went to bed that night more worried than ever. Millie and Max seemed to sense that and decided to sleep in my room. Sensibly, Millie lay on the floor alongside my bed. Max tried to get in beside me. Finally, he settled for the bottom of the bed, laying his head on my feet. It took me ages to get to sleep and, when I did, I dreamed of dark woods where Beachbabe was chasing Flip. I was chasing Beachbabe, yelling at her to leave Flip alone, when I stumbled and fell. I tried to get up and found that I could hardly breathe, found that I was choking, found that I was being pushed down and down and down. I wakened up with a start and found Max lying on my chest, snoring gently. I rolled him off.

It was still early, but already the bright morning light had found a chink in my curtains and a strip of sunshine illuminated one wall. I got up and pulled back the curtains. I could see Ben Bracken in the distance, its lower slopes covered in pine forest. Lower still were the indigenous trees: rowan, oak and silver birch. They were covered in bright green leaves at the moment, but, come autumn, the leaves would change to glorious reds and golds and the birds would have a feast on the rowan berries. I sighed. Auchtertuie was a wonderful place to live. Why did some people want to spoil it? Why couldn't they leave us and the animals alone?

I looked down at the pens and runs. All was quiet. At least the animals had slept better than I had. Then I looked again. The carefully secured doors to the pens and runs were open. That shouldn't be. I stuck my feet into my old slippers and flew downstairs, Millie and Max at my heels. I turned the lock on the kitchen door and ran out into the yard.

It was silent. No barking dogs to greet me. No Donk. No Lily.

The dogs and donkeys had all disappeared!

Chapter 19

I ran back inside the inn. 'Dad!' I yelled. 'Dad!'

My voice must have conveyed my panic, because Dad, Archie and Roderick came running.

'What is it, Kat?' Dad asked, his hair still tousled from sleep. 'Are you all right?'

'The donkeys have disappeared,' I said tearfully. 'And the dogs. They've all gone.'

The four of us hurried out to the yard and checked the pens and runs. The locks had been broken and the animals were nowhere to be seen.

'I bet this is another way of trying to force us out of business,' said Dad grimly. 'If people can't trust us with their animals . . . if they don't think they're safe . . .'

The only boarders left were the rabbits, the guinea pigs and Emily. Whoever had let the donkeys and dogs loose hadn't been brave enough to go near the tarantula. Emily ran about her vivarium rather frantically. She knew something was wrong. I forced myself to be calm and opened up her vivarium. She ran up my arm.

'It's OK, Emily,' I said. 'It's OK. At least you're safe. I don't know what we'd have told your family if you'd disappeared.'

'But what are we going to tell the others?' said Dad. 'We must set up a search party right away. I'll phone Constable Ross. Get dressed, everyone, we're going to need all the help we can get.'

I threw on my jeans and sweatshirt and Archie and I searched the shoreline while Dad and Roderick scoured the woods at the back of the inn. Dad had phoned Constable Ross, who promised to come as quickly as he could, but a climber had been reported missing on Ben Bracken, and Constable Ross was going out with the mountain rescue team to look for him. The Ben can be treacherous, even in summer. When the mist comes down it's easy to lose your way.

The water of the loch looked friendly enough in the early morning. Sunlight danced off the wavelets and, further out, the buoys marking the lobster pots nodded their friendly orange heads. But I knew the loch had its dark side. I knew how deep it was. I knew how dangerous the currents could be. Supposing whoever had let the animals loose had taken them out there and . . . I pushed the thought away. We just had to find them. Archie and I trudged over patches of sand, slithered over rocks and searched every nook and cranny, every little wooded inlet we could think of, but we found nothing.

'I don't think they were brought this way, Kat.' Archie was thoughtful. 'There are no hoof or paw prints.'

I tried to stop panicking and think logically.

'You're right,' I said. 'I think we're wasting our time here. Let's go back to the inn and see if the others have had any luck.'

When we got back, Kirsty was there, furiously baking pancakes. She was clearly upset by the news.

'What kind of people would even think to do such a thing?' she said. 'Just let me get my hands on them and I'll give them something to think about.' And she waved her big wooden spoon in the air, covering us all in pancake batter.

I went to the reception desk and brought back the big map Dad uses to direct tourists to places of interest. I spread it out on the kitchen table while Archie spread home-made strawberry jam on the pancakes. I was racking my brains for inspiration when Dad and Roderick came back. One look at their faces told me they'd had no luck either. Neither had Donald, who'd met up with them and gone looking too.

Morag hurried in with the post. We didn't need to tell her what had happened. News travels fast in Auchtertuie.

'There will be a search party here in half an hour,' she said.

Dad looked at the map spread out on the table.

'If we could think like the criminals who did this,' he said, 'we might be able to decide what they did with the animals. If they're not in the forest they must have been loaded into a van at the back of the inn and taken somewhere else. They can't just have disappeared into thin air.'

While the rest of us pored over the map, Morag sat down to have her usual cup of tea. We were so intent upon our task we didn't notice her go stiff and glassy-eyed, but we did notice when the cup fell from her fingers and smashed on to the kitchen floor.

'What on earth?' said Kirsty, then stopped. 'Listen. Perhaps she sees something.'

When Morag spoke, her voice was very distant and strange.

'The loch,' she said.

'Oh no.' I could feel the colour drain from my face and I clutched the edge of the table.

'A cave on the lochside. I see a cave on the lochside and I feel . . . fear, fear. Terrible fear.' And Morag shivered uncontrollably.

'Smugglers' Cave,' I yelled. 'The animals are in Smugglers' Cave!'

'But that's miles away,' said Dad. 'I don't know . . . how can we be sure . . . ?'

Morag came out of her trance. 'What happened?' she said, still shaking. 'Was I any help?'

'Yes, yes,' I said and hugged her. 'I'm sure you were. But we must head for Smugglers' Cave right now. The tide's on the turn, and if we don't get there soon, the animals will drown.'

Chapter 20

My dad is usually a careful driver. He worries about wildlife crossing the roads and drives slowly, but not that morning. That morning, Ali McAlly would have been proud of him. Dad climbed into our old van, put his foot down and went into racing driver mode. Archie and I hung on. We'd left Kirsty and Morag back at the inn, phoning all the volunteer searchers to come, in whatever vehicle they could, to Smugglers' Cave. Roderick followed us in his hire car and, as we hurtled along the snaky road that bordered the lochside, we could see an odd assorted line of vehicles behind us. There was Jinty in her little white baker's van, Morag in the post van, Donald in his open-topped jeep, Ali McAlly in his battered old taxi and, bringing up the rear, Aeneas McCrumble's big removal van with 'NO LOAD TOO BIG OR TOO SMALL' painted in large letters on the side. It was Auchtertuie's version of the cavalry.

'Just look at all these folks who have come to help,' said Archie.

'This is a small community,' said Dad. 'We try to help each other if we can. That's how it works, most of the time.'

When we came upon traffic, Dad leaned on his horn. People seemed to realise there was an emergency and pulled into the nearest passing place. Dad gave them a 'thank you' toot and Archie and I waved as we passed. We waved at someone else, too. Out on the loch, Lachy McCrumble in his fishing boat was doing his best to keep up with us.

We reached the turn-off for Smugglers' Cave and bumped down the unmade road. The springs on our old van were a bit dodgy and our heads bounced off the roof. Not that we cared. Dad took the van as close as he dared to the shore then we leapt out and started running. I knew the way because I'd visited the cave lots of times before, mostly with tourists. We reached the shore and turned right. The cave lay about a quarter of a mile away over a very rocky beach.

'Be careful,' warned Dad. 'We don't need any broken ankles right now.'

He was right, but it wasn't easy keeping upright on the seaweed-slippy stones.

I leapt ahead. I was more used to this than Dad or Archie. I rounded a high outcrop of rocks and, at last, the cave came in sight. The tide had turned and water was running strongly into it.

'Be careful, Kat,' called Dad again. 'Remember the pull of the undercurrents.'

But I had speeded up even more, careless of the dense seaweed carpet, careless of the swirling water round me. I was convinced Morag was right. I was sure the animals were there. My jeans grew heavy with the seawater, which reached almost to my knees as I entered the cave. It was dim, the daylight only penetrating a little way. I switched on my torch, repaired with Sellotape after its accident in the woods. I shone it around. Nothing. I waded further into the cave. Water buffeted and tugged at my legs.

'Donk,' I called. 'Lily, Seamus, Brandy, Ginger, can you hear me?'

Nothing. Just the sound of the loch as it rushed into the cave. I stumbled over a hidden rock and fell. Salt water gushed into my nose and mouth making me gasp and choke.

I tried again. 'Donk, Lily, Seamus, Brandy, Ginger, are you there?'

The tide sucked back out of the cave and for a few seconds it was quiet. Then I heard it. A faint, terrified bark.

'They're here,' I yelled at the splashing figures behind me. 'They're here!'

I rounded a bend in the cave. We were deep underground by this time and the beam of my torch bounced off eerie green walls that had never seen the light of day. Then I saw the animals. They were tethered together to an iron ring in the wall. Tethered and left to drown.

Tears of anger stung my eyes as I waded towards them as fast as I could. I talked all the time in a reassuring voice and called all of them by name. I reached Donk first. He was trembling with fear and cold. I thought of all he had suffered before and I trembled with rage. I kept talking to the animals as I worked at the ropes that held them fast. The ropes were thick and the salt water made them stiff and difficult to undo. Dad and Archie reached me and Dad took over on the ropes while Archie and I soothed and cuddled the animals as best we could. We held Brandy and Ginger, the two smallest, above the rising tide.

'Got it.' Dad gave a sigh of relief as the knotted

rope started to loosen. He hauled at the rope as a long line of people, sensibly roped together, appeared behind us. The Auchtertuie cavalry had arrived.

Giving each other support against the tugging, swirling tide, we managed to half lead, half carry the shivering animals out of the cave and over the rocks to safety.

I'll never forget that moment. We all collapsed, panting, on to a little patch of sand, completely exhausted.

Dad and I recovered quickly and examined the animals. They seemed physically unharmed, just terrified by their ordeal. Donk was especially wild-eyed and anxious. I stood with my arms about his neck. 'You're all right, Donk. You're safe now,' I whispered over and over again in his ear. Eventually he calmed down a little and we were able to coax him into Aeneas McCrumble's big furniture van. Aeneas had a pile of old sheets and blankets that he used to protect the furniture he moved, and we piled these on to Donk and Lily to keep them warm and safe on the journey home. I travelled with them.

The dogs were supposed to go home with Dad, but they decided to follow me into the big van instead. So did Archie. It was a bit like Noah's Ark on wheels. Brandy and Ginger were quite lively on the way home. I suppose they were used to great escapes. But Seamus was jittery. He looked at us with his big soulful eyes as if to say, 'Why would anyone want to do this to us?' I sat on a heap of blankets and cuddled him. He slid forward on to my wet knees like a giant puppy. I don't know if you've ever had a fully grown Irish wolfhound on your lap, but Archie said you could hardly see me behind him.

The little line of assorted vehicles made its way slowly back to Auchtertuie. Lachy McCrumble gave us a toot from his foghorn as we went. He had witnessed the rescue from his boat, and it suddenly dawned on me that, if we had been very much later, the animals would have drowned, and Lachy might have had to pick up the bodies. I shivered and cuddled Seamus even closer.

When we reached home, we unloaded the animals and took them all into the kitchen where it was warm. We made sure they were dry and comfortable and Kirsty fed them doggy and donkey treats. Everyone made a great fuss of them till we were sure they were feeling better.

Then Constable Ross appeared. It was so crowded, he could hardly get in through the kitchen door.

'I heard what happened,' he said, 'but I had to go with the rescue team.'

I immediately felt bad. I'd completely forgotten about the lost climber.

'The climber's safe,' he said, 'but he'd slipped on some loose scree and fallen and broken his leg. We had to stretcher him down and get him to the cottage hospital. He has mild hypothermia, but he'll be OK.'

Everyone nodded, glad it had turned out all right. The Ben had claimed a few lives in the past.

'Now you'd better tell me what all this is about,' said Constable Ross, scratching Donk's head.

We all started talking at once. Constable Ross held up his hands and got out his official police notebook. 'One at a time, if you please,' he said.

'I think Kat should begin,' said Dad. 'She was the one who discovered that the dogs and donkeys had disappeared.'

'Well,' I said. 'It all started when I had this terrible dream . . .'

Chapter 21

Dad slept in the back yard after that. He put a folding bed in Donk's little shed and slept with the donkeys. I wanted to do it, but Dad wouldn't let me.

'No, Kat,' he said. 'If these villains come back, I want to be here.' He had his mobile phone with him and promised to contact Constable Ross if there were any strange noises in the night. But I know he hardly slept. None of us did, we were so busy listening out for trouble. I started being scared of normal night sounds: the hoot of a barn owl, the bark of a fox, even seagulls landing on the roof had me leaping out of bed. Then, one morning, really early, I heard a tapping on my window.

Help, someone's trying to get in, I thought, and pretended to be still asleep. After a moment or two, I cautiously half opened one eye and took a peek. The tapping continued, but it wasn't a burglar. It was a huge crow. He had seen his reflection in the window and thought it was another crow. He was pecking at it, trying to chase it off. I got up and shooed him away, but my heart was thumping madly in my chest and there was no way I could go back to sleep.

After a few days of watching and waiting and jumping at every sound, we had another kitchen table meeting. Constable Ross was there. He was still making enquiries about the disappearance of the animals.

'I have no proof of anything,' he said. 'No proof at all, but I have some very strong suspicions.'

'Oh?' We all leaned forward.

Constable Ross looked at us, then looked at his watch. 'End of my shift. I'm off duty now,' he said, and took off his hat. He smiled round the table at Dad, Roderick, Archie, Donald, Jinty, Morag, Kirsty and me. 'Now I'm Willie Ross and not Constable Ross,' he said, 'and Willie Ross has some gossip.'

Gossip? Auchtertuie loved gossip. We leaned forward even further.

'On the morning of the animals' disappearance,

my dad was delivering some meat to the big hotel on the estate. He came across a large van parked outside the kitchen premises. It was being thoroughly hosed down. Nothing unusual in that, you might say, but Dad did notice something else. He noticed a man sweeping out manure from the back of the van into a bucket.

'The man saw Dad looking.

' "Been transporting some elk on to the estate," the man said. "Just clearing up the mess." But Dad said what was in that bucket hadn't come from any elk. He knows what elk dung looks like—'

'Brownish black, just over a centimetre in diameter, a bit like a cherry,' volunteered Archie.

Oh help, now that boy was an expert on poo as well!

Willie Ross nodded. 'But that wasn't what was in the bucket. It looked more like donkey dung to Dad.'

Willie Ross glanced round the table. 'As Constable Ross I investigated, of course, but there was no proof of anything, and only Dad's word for what he saw. There was no way the law could take the matter further. That's the gossip.'

And Willie Ross sipped his tea and said no more.

We all looked at one another.

'Well, thank you for passing on that bit of gossip,

Willie,' said Dad. 'We'll have to think about that.'

'THINK about it?' I jumped to my feet. 'We'll have to DO something about it. We can't let them, whoever THEY are, get away with what they did.'

'Calm down, Kat,' said Dad. 'You heard what Constable Ross said about proof. We can't take the law into our own hands.'

'That's right,' said Willie Ross. 'The law would have to not know about it, if you did. The law would have to be elsewhere at the time.' And Willie Ross looked at his watch again. 'Och no, is that the time already? I must away now for I've an early start tomorrow. Did I tell you I'm off to a conference in Inverness? I'll be away for about two days, and no one here to cover for me either.' And he picked up his hat. 'I'll say goodnight, then,' he smiled, and left.

Everybody round the table raised their eyebrows and grinned. Good old Willie.

'OK,' I said. 'We've got forty-eight hours. If C.P. Associates think they can drive us out of the Crumbling Arms, they're very much mistaken. But we need a plan and quickly.'

'Nothing violent,' said Donald immediately. 'I won't be a party to anything violent.'

'There will be no violence,' said Dad. 'Of any sort.'

'Oh.' Kirsty eyed the broom and looked despondent. Roderick cracked his knuckles sadly.

'What we need to do is think sneaky like they do,' said Archie.

'I'm racking my brains,' said Morag, 'but I'm not very good with sneaky.'

I thought about how I had sneaked into the big hotel to have a look at what was happening when it was being built. I knew all the ways in and out of the hotel. I knew my way around the grounds. I could do sneaky.

'Em.' I cleared my throat. 'Maybe you'll think I'm crazy. Probably you'll think I'm nuts. But I think I may have a plan that might work.'

Chapter 22

Everyone looked at me. All the faces were interested and expectant, except Dad's. His face was wary. In the past, not all of my plans had worked. Like my plan to make tablet and sell it to the guests to earn extra pocket money. I'm sure I put the right amount of butter, sugar and milk into the pot, and I brought it to the boil and stirred it for ages, but somehow the tablet turned out a little firmer than it ought, and one of our guests broke a front tooth on it and had to call out the emergency dentist. Then there was my plan to go carol singing, even though it wasn't Christmas. I did earn some extra money, singing outside folk's houses, but only because they paid me to go away.

'Is this a sensible plan, Kat?' Dad asked.

'No,' I answered truthfully, 'but it's the only one I can think of at the moment, and, unless anyone else has a better idea . . .' I looked round the table. There was silence.

'OK,' I said. 'C.P. Associates have been sneakily trying to put us out of business. Right?'

Everyone nodded.

'Well, two can play at that game. I think we should try to do the same to them. They tried to make it look as though our animals had escaped, so supposing it *appeared* that our animals had escaped again, only this time they turn up at the big hotel on the estate? The dogs love to go swimming, so, supposing they decided to join the guests in the outdoor pool? And what if Flip got the smell of cat food coming from the hotel dining room? He could join the guests in there. Donk and Lily would just love the tasty flower-beds in front of the hotel, and Emily might just go walkabout and end up on Beachbabe's pillow. All that would cause a bit of a stushie, and dent the big hotel's reputation, don't you think?'

'I like it,' cried Roderick. 'It's a bold plan, Kat.'

'I like it too,' grinned Archie, 'especially that last bit about Beachbabe.'

'It's a good plan,' said Kirsty, 'because it would

look as though whoever abducted the animals in the first place had come back to have another go, only this time the animals got away. We could blame it on the abductors without actually having any proof of who they were.'

'I could lead us through the estate quite undetected,' said Donald, 'and Kat knows the layout of the hotel.'

'It *is* a good plan,' said Morag. 'I can feel it in my bones.'

Dad shook his head in disbelief. 'It's a crazy plan,' he said. 'There are all sorts of things that could go wrong, and we could get caught and end up in court. I just can't ask you to risk it. This is *my* problem. Perhaps I could do some of the things Kat talked about, on my own.'

Everyone looked at him.

'Don't be so daft, Hector,' said Kirsty.

'This is McCrumble business and we're all McCrumbles,' said Morag.

'Hear, hear,' everyone agreed, and Dad was simply outvoted.

I grinned at him. 'It'll be fine, Dad. And it's much better than just sitting here waiting for C.P. Associates to order up another dirty trick. We have to seize the initiative, take the battle into enemy territory, beat them at their own game.'

Roderick looked at me in amazement. 'Is she always this fierce?' he asked Dad.

'This is nothing,' said Dad. 'You should see what she's like if someone beats her at Scrabble.'

I grinned. Dad was won over. Now to put the plan into action. We only had two days until the 'law' came back. We would have to move fast.

Donald fetched Dad's map of the area and spread it out on the kitchen table.

'This is the best route through the estate to the hotel,' he said, tracing it with a long brown forefinger. 'This way will give us plenty of cover, but there is one big problem – we'll have to travel at night, and we could run into the badger baiters. Don't forget they're still out there. They haven't been caught.'

There was a glum silence while everyone thought about that. I hadn't forgotten about them, but the worry over the other animals had pushed them to one side for the moment. Then I remembered a telly programme I had seen.

'Disinformation,' I cried. 'We need to spread disinformation. Morag will be perfect for that.'

'Disinformation? Is that the same as gossip?' asked Morag. 'I'm good at that.'

I nodded. 'Just tell people when you're out on your rounds that you've heard that Constable Ross isn't really away to Inverness for a conference at all but has gathered a police team together with tracker dogs to hunt for the badger baiters. If you swear everyone to secrecy, it'll be round the entire area in no time. That should keep the badger baiters in their beds for a couple of nights.'

'Och, I can do that right enough, Kat,' said Morag. 'No problem.'

'You have a very devious mind, Kat McCrumble,' grinned Roderick. 'I'm glad I'm on your side.'

'It is a good idea,' said Donald. 'But we'll keep a sharp lookout just the same.'

'We'll have to decide who's responsible for each of the animals,' said Dad. 'We must make sure they will come to no harm, otherwise the plan is off.'

'I'll look after Flip,' I said. 'He knows me best.'

'I think Emily likes me,' said Archie. 'And I know a lot about spiders.'

I grinned at him. He just wanted to see Beachbabe's face when she was confronted by a tarantula.

'I'll look after Millie and Max and the rest of the dogs,' said Roderick. 'They know me really well by now.'

'Especially since you buy them chocolate every morning when you go for your paper!' I said.

'OK, that leaves Donald and me to look after Donk and Lily,' said Dad.

'But what about us?' complained Jinty and Kirsty. 'What can we do? Who do we get to look after? Don't we get to come?'

'No,' I said. 'The bakery and the inn have to open as usual. It'll be too obvious if we all disappear at once.'

'Quite right, Kat,' Dad agreed. 'Everything has to appear normal.'

Normal? In Auchtertuie? He had to be kidding.

Chapter 23

I couldn't wait for the next night to come. All day long I was in a state, doing stupid things. Like putting the wrong washing powder into the dishwasher after lunch. Kirsty came back from the shops to find the kitchen floor covered in bubbles and the dishwasher quietly hiccuping in the corner. She gave a yell and Archie and I hurried to investigate. We'd been in the lounge arguing over a game of Scrabble.

'You can't spell colour without a "u",' I told him. 'Even if that is the American spelling.'

'You can't have "shooglie" then, either,' he declared.

'But shooglie's a real word. It's a lovely word. You

can have a shooglie tooth or a shooglie table. It's Scottish for "wobbly". Ask anyone.'

But when we heard Kirsty yell, we jumped up so fast we upset the Scrabble board, so we'll never know who would have won.

We found Kirsty up to her knees in bubbles.

'Someone, who shall be nameless, Katriona McCrumble,' she said, 'doesn't have her mind on what she's doing today.'

'Sorry,' I said, as I watched Kirsty wade through the bubbles to put away the shopping. 'But you don't usually keep the toilet rolls in the fridge, either.'

'Tsk,' said Kirsty, and removed them to their usual cupboard beside the window.

'I'll get rid of these bubbles for you, Kirsty,' said Archie, and began leaping about the kitchen, jumping on as many as he could. It looked like fun so Kirsty and I joined in. Millie and Max heard our laughter and arrived to play too, chasing the bubbles around the room and snapping at those which escaped into the air. Then Kirsty opened the back door and tried to sweep the bubbles out into the yard. Donk and Lily looked up and became fascinated by these strange, floating circles.

'Hee haw.' They trotted round after them. That set off the rest of the canine boarders, and before long, the yard was full of barking and bubbles. There was so much noise we didn't hear Dad come back from Inverness with the supplies.

'What on earth . . . ?' he said when he saw the yard.

'Just a little mistake with the soap powder, Hector,' said Kirsty. 'None of us is thinking straight today because of . . . you know what . . .'

'Well, you'd better get a grip of yourselves,' said Dad. 'We can't afford to have anyone doing silly things.'

At that moment the phone rang and Kirsty hurried indoors to answer it.

She came back grinning. 'That was Roderick. He phoned to say he'll be on the four o'clock bus. It seems someone took him to Inverness today and forgot to bring him back.'

'Oh no,' gasped Dad. 'He went to the library while I went to the cash and carry. I was supposed to pick him up again, but I was so busy thinking about other things, I completely forgot.'

'Well,' I grinned. 'You'd better get a grip of yourself, Dad. We can't afford to have anyone doing silly things.'

Dad smiled and shook his head. 'On the way home I saw Donald coming out of the chippy munching a black pudding supper. He hates black pudding. He's not thinking straight either.'

After dinner that night, it was my turn to spread a map out on the table. I hadn't drawn it to scale, but it had all the necessary details of the hotel on it, like the locations of the swimming pool, the main dining room and Beachbabe's bedroom.

'Luckily, it's on the ground floor with a door on to a little veranda,' said Roderick. 'I found it easily when I went to see her. But how are we going to get Emily inside? If I know Beachbabe, the door will be locked.'

'I can open most doors,' volunteered Archie. 'I'm very good at picking locks.'

His father looked at him in amazement.

'Is that what they teach you at that fancy boarding school that costs me so much?' he said.

'It's not what they teach, but it's what I learned,' grinned Archie. 'My best friend Harry's father is a big-time crook. When Harry was little his baby-sitters were all burglars and safe-crackers and con men, so he knows loads of dodges. He taught me how to pick locks. That's how I can sneak down to the school kitchen at night and raid the fridge.'

Good old Archie. So he did know something useful after all.

'The tricky bit will be getting Emily back after Beachbabe's seen her,' I said.

'Not really,' said Archie. 'I'll leave the door open. Beachbabe will scream and run out. Then I'll just nip back in and retrieve Emily. Simple.'

I hoped so.

'Turning Donk and Lily loose on the flower-beds will be no problem,' said Dad. 'They only need moments to create havoc, then we'll call them back.'

'And the dogs will enjoy their swim,' smiled Donald. 'You've got the really tricky bit, Kat, getting Flip into the dining room.'

'I think I'll be all right,' I said. 'There are French doors that lead on to the terrace. Archie can unlock these for me, and I'll slip in and hide a little bit of cat food under the tables. On the way out I'll leave the doors slightly open for Flip to get inside, and I'll leave a trail of cat food from the edge of the forest to the dining room. He'll easily follow that. Once he's eaten, he'll go back into the forest like he always does. I'll be watching anyway to see that he's OK.'

'I don't know,' said Dad, running a worried hand through his hair. 'It'll all so risky. There's so much that could go wrong. Supposing we're caught.'

'Then we're looking for our animals that someone has let loose again. What could be more natural than that? We'll leave the pens and runs open like they were when the animals were abducted.'

'You have the makings of a fine criminal mind, Kat McCrumble,' said Dad.

'Thank you,' I grinned.

'You should meet my friend, Harry,' said Archie. 'He's taught me a thing or two about burglar alarms as well.'

'I'd like to meet him,' I said. 'I'd like to visit the USA. Perhaps I'll think about it when this caper is over.'

Chapter 24

The animals were still frisky after the bubbles incident, so I thought I'd better have a chat with them and tell them what was going on.

Some people think it's crazy talking to animals, but if you're an animal person you'll know it's not. I'm not suggesting they understand every word I say, but I'm sure they understand the feeling behind the words. I think they know if I'm happy or excited or sad. I'm sure that communicates itself. That's my theory anyway.

So I talked to the animals. I gathered them all together in Donk's pen, sat on an upturned bucket and had a word.

'You know we've been having problems at the

inn,' I said. 'Some nasty people are trying to force us out, so they can have the inn for themselves.'

I paused to look at them. They were all paying close attention apart from Max, who was scratching his ear with his back paw.

'Well, we're not going to be driven out by anyone, especially people who would steal animals and leave them . . .' I was going to say to drown, but I didn't want to upset them again . . . 'And leave them . . . for us to rescue. So, we're going to fight back, and we need your help. Is that OK? Will you help us?'

By this time Lily was rubbing her neck on the fence post and Donk was investigating the hole in the sleeve of my jersey. Seamus had sat down, put his head on my lap and was half asleep. Brandy and Ginger were trying to escape by tunnelling out of Donk's pen. Only Millie was paying any heed at all. I went into my pocket and brought out two carrots and a packet of doggy chocs. All of a sudden I had their undivided attention. Donk stopped unravelling my sweater, Seamus wakened up and licked my knees, clearly visible through my frayed jeans, and Max tried to steal the doggy chocs from my hand. I pushed him away gently.

'Now, listen carefully, all of you,' I whispered. 'This is top secret information and not to be divulged to anyone. Tonight, when everyone else is asleep, we're going to slip through the forest and head for the big hotel on the estate. When we get there we're going to have some fun. There's a lovely swimming pool for dogs and some beautiful flower-beds for donkeys. Emily and Flip will be with us too. Now, paws or hooves up anyone who doesn't want to come.'

All paws and hooves stayed firmly on the ground.

'Good,' I beamed. 'It'll be fun.'

'Can I come too?' said a voice behind me. 'I didn't know you spoke donkey, Kat. I never got past clementary dog myself. Listen. RUFF. RUFF. RUFF RUFF RUFF. That means, please may I have a choccy drop?'

I threw one. Archie caught it neatly and gave it to Seamus.

'Good boy, Archie,' I grinned, 'but just wait till you hear me speak spider and badger.'

That night I fetched Emily in her little box and sat down at the kitchen table to wait for Flip.

Supposing he doesn't come, I thought. Supposing his wife has got fed up with him going to the pub every night and has made him stay home to watch the kids, while she goes out with the girls. Or, supposing he's not feeling too well, and Mrs Flip has brought him in a nice bed of fresh grass and said, "Have a lie-down, dear, and you'll soon feel better." Or, supposing he's gone off chicken liver cat food. Or, supposing . . .

The cat flap opened and Flip poked his head in, then squeezed his body through.

'Hullo, Flip,' I sighed with relief, 'it's good to see you. We have a plan to get back at the bad guys tonight and I need your help.'

But Flip wasn't listening. He was investigating Samantha's food dish. He couldn't believe it was empty. He walked round and round it. But that didn't help, it was still empty. He lifted his black snout and sniffed the air. Ah ha, he could still smell chicken liver. It must be here somewhere. He padded across the floor to me. He could tell the smell was stronger here, and he was right. I had emptied several cans of cat food into poly bags and put them into my backpack. I got up and wandered round the room. Flip followed me. I picked up Emily in her box and walked out into the back yard. Flip followed me. Flip would follow me as long as I had chicken liver cat food.

The others were ready to go. Archie took charge of Emily, and the line of assorted humans – Dad, Archie, Roderick, Donald and I – with assorted animals – Donk, Lily, Seamus, Brandy and Ginger, Millie and Max and Flip – all set off on our adventure.

'Are we mad?' I whispered to Archie, as we slipped across the back yard, past the bird table and out into the forest.

'Completely,' said Archie, 'but it's fantastic. Just wait till I tell everyone back home.'

'I wish we were back home,' I said. 'I just hope everything goes according to plan.'

'Do you have another plan if it doesn't?'

'Yes,' I said, but didn't tell him it was entirely made up of running away very quickly.

Chapter 25

Luckily it was a fine night. The air was soft and still and smelt faintly of seaweed. Moonlight filtered through the trees as Donald led us further and further into the forest. Nobody said much, and when they did they spoke in whispers. All the animals were on leads apart from Millie, who scouted ahead of Donald. Dad had attached a little luminous strip to her collar so the light from our torches could pick her up.

We had all come well prepared with lightweight rucksacks Kirsty had packed. We had food and water for the animals and food and flasks of tea for ourselves, as well as spare batteries for the torches. Kirsty had also put in bandages and sticking plasters.

'Just in case you trip in the dark,' she said, then added, 'I wish I was coming with you. I won't sleep a wink tonight.'

I didn't think I would sleep either, though the plan was to rest for a while under the shelter of a huge overhanging rock that Donald knew well. My insides were hollow with excitement as I fell in at the rear of our little column. I kept turning round to make sure Flip was behind me. When we stopped at the overhang I would give him a little of the cat food from the backpack. Enough to keep him interested, but not too much in case he went home.

We trudged on for ages. The animals seemed quite happy. They were with people they knew and trusted. I just hoped that Morag's disinformation had worked and that we wouldn't run into the badger baiters. But the forest was quiet, apart from the usual night rustlings. Millie came face to face with a little roe deer at one point, but it melted into the forest as soon as it saw us. Owls called to each other and the odd bat flitted by, but nothing out of the ordinary. Except us. I began to imagine that the owls were gossiping about us.

'TWIT. Here, Mollie, came and take a look at this strange lot. I wonder what they're doing out here at this time of night.'

'TWOO, Ollie. They should all be home in their beds like decent human beings, not roaming the forest looking for trouble. I blame television myself, giving them all sorts of weird ideas. No good will come of it, you mark my words.'

If they were saying that, I hoped they were wrong.

After what seemed an age trying to avoid tree roots and low branches, Donald called a halt.

'We're nearly at the overhang,' he whispered. 'There's a lot of moss underneath it. Be careful not to slip.'

We gave the animals some food and water and made ourselves as comfortable as possible in the shelter of the rock. The animals all lay down, except Flip, who was used to being out at night. He prowled around close by. The humans huddled together and talked.

'So far, so good,' said Dad. 'The animals have been fantastic.'

'That's because they trust you, Hector,' said Roderick. 'Funnily enough, I found out in my researches that Old Hamish was good with animals. Apparently the local folks used to bring their sick animals to him, too.'

Dad nodded. 'Kat's even better with them than I am. Funny how history repeats itself.'

'Yeah.' Roderick paused. 'In my case it's with

marriage. My father was married six times and it looks like I'm headed the same way.'

'Is it all over with you and Beachbabe?' asked Dad.

'It should never have started. I just got so angry when Archie's mom married again that I decided I would show her I could do it too.'

'But five times,' said Dad. 'That's a lot of anger.'

'I know, and most of it directed at myself. I was crazy to lose Archie's mom, but I was just so stubborn at the time.'

'What made you break up?'

Oh oh, I thought, and they say females are nosy! But Dad was doing a really good job, so I carried on listening in.

'We broke up over dog food,' sighed Roderick.

'Dog food?' Dad was incredulous.

'Yeah. Crazy or what? We had a dog called Butch. He had been my dog till I married Archie's mom, then he kinda transferred his affections. Probably because he saw more of her than me. I was away on business most of the time. Anyway, one day I came home bringing Archie a toy car and Butch a couple of cans of his favourite dog food. Archie liked the car, but my wife wouldn't give the food to the dog. Said Butch hadn't eaten that kind of food for ages. Said she'd taken him to the vet with stomach problems and the vet had told her to feed him a different diet. I said I hadn't noticed. She said it was because I was never around. We rowed some, so she left and took Archie and the dog with her . . . I really missed them.'

I swallowed a lump in my throat and heard Archie sniff. He was obviously listening too.

The men fell silent. Max wormed his way on to Dad's lap and went to sleep. Brandy and Ginger curled up round each other and snored. Seamus slept beside Donk and Lily. I suppose he was nearer their size. Of all the domestic animals, only Millie was awake. She stood guard, head up, ears erect, listening. The moon slid over the treetops and briefly illuminated our little group. We looked like something out of my infant school nativity play. You could feel the excitement in the air. Only Donald seemed calm, but he was at home in the forest at any time.

'Can I ask you something, Donald?' asked Roderick suddenly.

'Ask away,' said Donald.

'Why are you a druid?'

'Because it's what I want to be and because it makes me happy. Are you happy?'

'Not really,' said Roderick.

'Then find out what makes you happy and do it.'

'I might just take your advice,' smiled Roderick.

Then everyone was silent. I think I must have dozed off because the next thing I knew, Dad was shaking me gently.

'Time to go, Kat. Donald says, if we leave now, we'll be in position by dawn, then we can stay hidden till breakfast time, and the great invasion.'

We all got to our feet, stretched and fell back into formation. It was colder now and we were glad to be moving. After what seemed an age, Donald called a halt in a little clearing.

'We'll wait here till it's time to go,' he smiled. 'Now it's over to you, Kat, for a quick revision of the invasion plan.'

I gulped and got out the map of the hotel I had drawn. I just hoped my memory of the layout was as good as I thought it was.

Chapter 26

We stayed hidden in the forest till almost dawn. I was shivering with fear and anticipation. Finally it was time to go. Archie and I slipped through a five-barred gate and into the hotel grounds. All was quiet. We skirted the flower-beds and the ornamental fountain and mounted the wide stairs of the terrace to the French doors of the dining room. Archie set to work on the lock with a long pin. I watched impatiently. Fingers of dawn were already lightening the sky and I was anxious to get on with our plan.

'Stand still,' hissed Archie. 'You're putting me off.'

I bit back a retort and stopped hopping from

foot to foot. He almost had the doors open when a sudden noise made us flatten ourselves on the ground.

'What was that?' whispered Archie.

Cautiously I raised my head. A solitary heron had landed on the ornamental fountain and was eyeing up the carp for his breakfast.

'It's OK,' I said. 'Just a hungry heron.'

Archie resumed his lock picking. A sudden click and . . . success! We were in.

While Archie slipped away to unpick the lock on Beachbabe's door, I opened up my bag of cat food. Bent double in case I was spotted, I put some under each of the breakfast tables. The long, white, stiffly starched cloths hid the cat food perfectly. Then I left, leaving the door slightly ajar and scattering the rest of the food in a trail back to the forest.

'So far so good,' I said to Dad and Donald, who had been keeping Flip busy with a little cat food while I was away. I took over.

Dad and Donald moved off with Donk and Lily. The donkeys were frisky in the crisp morning air and smartly picked up their hooves. I watched as Dad and Donald led them through the gate and as far into the gardens as they dared. Then Donk spied the flower-beds and he was off, the faithful

Lily at his heels. Dad and Donald returned to our hiding place.

We waited till we could see the early morning swimmers arrive at the pool, then Roderick led the dogs to the bushes that grew alongside. We watched as he bent and took off their leads. That was all it needed. The dogs crashed through the bushes and did some spectacular dives into the pool. Millie leapt into the middle and doggy-paddled very precisely to the far end. Seamus jumped in beautifully and landed on a large float before rolling off into the water. Brandy and Ginger bounded in together and made a terrific splash, while Max took off like a rocket and landed on the head of a portly gentleman just coming up for air. I don't know who was more surprised, but Max thought it was a good game anyway. He scrabbled out of the pool and jumped in all over again. The noise was terrific. The swimmers yelled and screamed and hurriedly left the pool.

While all this was going on, I seized my chance to set Flip off on the cat food trail. He was up to the challenge. He snuffled and munched his way up to the terrace steps, climbed them with ease and found the open dining-room door. He stuck his nose inside, then, with a wiggle of his black rear, he disappeared.

I had to know what was happening. I couldn't resist it. I left my hiding place and crept up to the French doors. I stuck my nose in much like Flip had done. Guests were seated at the tables having breakfast, but where was Flip? I could see no sign. Then a table cover moved and a lady wearing more gold than Midas hissed at her husband.

'There's something touching my right leg.'

Her husband looked down at her leg.

'There's nothing there, Irma.'

'I tell you, something touched my leg.'

Her husband looked under the table, but, by this time, Flip had moved on.

'There's nothing there, Irma. Take another pill.'

Then a child at the next table became aware of Flip. He slid under the table to investigate, then sat back up again.

'There's a big black and white hairy thing down there having his breakfast too,' he said conversationally to his parents.

'That's nice, Charlie,' said his mum. 'Now eat up your muesli like a good boy.'

The child picked up his spoon and looked around.

'The big black and white hairy thing's crawled under the next table now.'

'What an imagination Charlie has,' his mum said

to his dad. 'Perhaps he'll be a famous author one day.'

I don't know what his dad replied because all of a sudden there was a yell from the next table.

'There's a badger! There's a badger!'

Flip had been discovered. People leapt up from their tables. Some jumped on to chairs. Crockery went flying, orange juice spilled, coffee grew cold.

Staff came running, looking for Flip. But Flip was a great dodger and as they looked under one table he was already under the next. He wasn't leaving while there was cat food to be had. He had walked a long way for it. But there was so much panic you'd have thought a posse of panthers had been let loose.

I sneaked away from my hiding place, scattering more cat food as I went. Flip caught the scent and headed back through the French doors and down the terrace steps after me. Two minutes later we were safely back in our hiding place. I let out a long sigh of relief.

That's when I heard the piercing yell. It could only have come from Beachbabe. She'd obviously found Emily. She appeared round the corner of the hotel, wearing nothing but a large blue bath towel, and flew past the dogs in the swimming pool.

'Help! Save me, save me! I'm being attacked by a giant spider! Help! Help!'

She wasn't being attacked by a giant spider because I could see Archie making his way stealthily back into the forest with Emily's box tucked underneath his arm.

'Wow!' he said breathlessly, flopping down beside me. 'You should have seen Beachbabe's face. Emily was magnificent. She did that little movement with her front legs like she was sharpening them and couldn't wait to tuck into Beachbabe. Fantastic fun.'

A faint whistle sounded and the dogs, including Max, left the swimming pool and disappeared into the bushes. Soon they appeared by our sides, happy and dripping. Max gave himself a good shake and soaked everyone.

'Good dogs. Good dogs,' said Roderick, panting after them. He took out a large bar of chocolate and handed it out to them. 'Just this one last time,' he said to me. He knew they weren't really allowed human chocolate. He also knew they loved it.

That just left Dad, Donald and the donkeys. As arranged, Dad strode in full view up to the hotel while Donald 'rescued' the donkeys from the flower-beds and brought them back to us.

Now, Dad was supposed to do this bit on his own. He was supposed to go into the hotel and demand to know why his animals had been taken from their home and found on hotel property. But, Dad is so nice, too nice sometimes. And supposing he forgot some of the things he had to say. And, well . . . I just wanted to be in on it anyway. I was still furious about the animals being taken to Smugglers' Cave. I handed the remaining cat food to Archie.

'Head back to the inn and keep Flip following you. I have a few things to say to the hotel people.'

Archie mumbled something which I didn't quite catch, but it sounded remarkably like 'Surprise, surprise.'

Chapter 27

I made as dramatic an entrance to the hotel as I could. Not easy through a revolving door. The hotel was even more luxurious than I remembered: deep sofas you could get lost in for ever, and more rugs than a Persian rug shop. I caught up with Dad as he passed the huge flower arrangement in the middle of the foyer. Ivy curled round masses of gold and pink roses and cascaded on to the floor. A little different to our vase of wild flowers on the reception table at the Crumbling Arms.

'What are you doing here?' asked Dad.

'I want to tell them what I think of them. You're much too polite,' I said.

Dad tutted but didn't send me away.

The girl at the long marble reception desk, whose tartan badge declared she was called 'Zandra', was very smiley.

'Good morning,' she said brightly, giving us the full benefit of her shiny red lippy which I noticed had come off on her teeth. 'Can I help you?'

'We'd like to speak to the manager, please,' said Dad.

See what I mean. Far too polite.

'The head guy. Mr C.P. Associate himself,' I added.

Red Lippy ignored me.

'I'm sorry,' she said to Dad, 'but it's not possible to see the manager without an appointment. Mr Coulter is in a meeting at the moment.'

'Then kindly get him out of it,' said Dad. 'This is very important.'

'I'm sorry.' Zandra's smile was completely insincere. 'That's just not possible.'

'Then it's possible this hotel will be sued for squillions of pounds,' I said. I wasn't exactly sure how much a squillion was, but it sounded a lot.

Before Zandra could reply, several hotel guests, some of them in bathrobes and some still clutching pieces of toast, erupted into the foyer, clamouring to see the manager too.

'I demand to know why the hotel swimming pool

is infested with mangy dogs this morning,' said one overfed lady with pink hair.

Mangy? I don't think so, madam. Hairy, perhaps. Smelly, probably. Thick as a plank in Max's case. But mangy? Definitely not.

'It is totally unhygienic. Who knows what they may have . . . deposited . . . in the water? And they probably have fleas!'

'You think that's bad? There was a wild badger in the dining room,' complained another.

'That would definitely have fleas. And there are donkeys eating up the flower-beds. When you think of what it costs to stay here and they let animals roam loose . . . it's a disgrace, that's what it is.'

'That's nothing,' screeched a familiar voice. 'There was a TARANTULA in my bedroom. I came out of the shower and there it was on my pillow. It was going to EAT me. I just KNOW it. I was lucky to escape with my life. My room is being searched, but it seems to have disappeared. Who knows where it is? I was afraid to put on these clothes in case it was LURKING.'

The people round about Beachbabe started to edge away, just in case, though the skimpy violet shorts she was wearing wouldn't have given Emily much cover. The high heels she had on seemed to be made out of clear plastic, held on by a strap of thin purple elastic. I'm sure I used to have a Barbie doll with shoes like that.

Zandra bit into her red lippy and wondered what to do. I helped her out.

'We want the manager,' I chanted. 'We want the manager.'

The irate hotel guests joined in.

'We want the manager. We want the manager.'

I don't think the hotel had ever witnessed anything like it. Possibly the manager hadn't either for he hurried out from a door behind the reception desk. He still had his breakfast napkin tucked into his shirt, and judging by the yellow stains on it, his important meeting had been with a runny boiled egg. He hurriedly pulled off the napkin and held up his hand for silence. Silly man. My PE teacher does that too and it doesn't work for her either. There was only one thing for it. I hauled myself up on to the reception desk, put my fingers to my lips, and gave my piercing dog whistle. That got everyone's attention and silenced them for a moment. One or two of them nearly came to heel.

'There are some things I think you should know about,' I said. 'My dad and I run the Crumbling Arms inn and animal sanctuary in the village, and someone is trying to force us out. There have been some really rotten tricks played on us at the inn, and a few days ago our animals were abducted. They were driven to a local cave and left to drown. We just managed to reach them before the tide did.'

The audience gasped.

'This morning,' I went on, 'our animals were gone again. We followed their tracks through the forest and found them here. What does this hotel want with them? What does it want with us? There's something very strange going on in this place.'

There was the sound of angry mutterings and sympathetic noises.

'I think the police should be informed,' said one man. 'There is obviously some dirty work afoot here. Abducting animals is an outrage.'

'I'll be packing my bags,' said another, 'and I won't be paying my bill. I shall report this entire matter to the tourist board.'

'And we won't be recommending this place to our friends,' muttered some others.

The manager was conciliatory. 'Please, ladies and gentlemen, please,' he said. 'I can assure you that nothing like this has ever happened before, and I can assure you it won't happen again. I'm so sorry you've been upset, but . . .'

But his apologies fell on deaf ears; his guests were leaving.

I jumped down from the reception desk and gave Dad my 'mission accomplished' wink. Dad nodded and we made our way through the crowd to the front door. I was so elated, I got inside the revolving door and pushed it too hard. It pushed back, whizzed me round, and I ended up back inside the foyer, facing the reception desk. The manager was talking to someone. I couldn't hear what he was saying, but he was giving someone a right telling-off, judging by the way he was stabbing his finger into the other man's chest. That someone was not enjoying the encounter. That someone's expression was as black as Ali McAlly's cat. That someone was Ron Jackson.

Chapter 28

Dad and I left the hotel and, when we were sure no one was looking, slipped back into the forest and caught up with the others. The animals, as well as the humans, were tired after all the excitement, and we had lots of stops for rests on the way home. We went via Flip's sett. Thankfully, the ground around it was undisturbed. No sign of any badger baiting. Flip immediately disappeared inside his sett, no doubt for a long sleep. I wondered if Mrs Flip would nag him . . .

'And just where do you think you've been all night? Off to see some bimbo badger, I shouldn't wonder.'

'Don't be silly, dear. I just had a wander through

the forest to try out that new hotel. The food's good, but it's a long way to go for a bite to eat and I'm tired out now. Got to get some sleep. Good morning. Zzzzz.'

I hoped Mrs Flip hadn't been too worried about him.

Kirsty had been worried about us. She was watching for us from the back door of the inn.

'Och, there you are at last,' she cried. 'I've been fretting, imagining all sorts. Morag was here earlier and went into one of her wee trances. Her blue eye told her you were all on your way back and everything was fine, but I wouldn't believe it till I saw you with my own eyes. Jinty's been on the phone too. Every two minutes. She was so concerned. It was a mad thing to be doing, Kat McCrumble.'

'I know,' I grinned, and hugged her. 'But we got away with it. The animals were fantastic. It was as if they just knew what they had to do. Now, put the kettle on and we'll be in as soon as we've fed the animals.'

Kirsty fed us too. She had a great cauldron of Scotch broth simmering on the hob and a batch of warm oatcakes to go with it. That wasn't all. Several chocolate cakes, plates of scones and pancakes, and enough millionaire shortbread to rot the teeth of the entire nation were piled up in the kitchen.

'I was so agitated, I had to keep myself busy,' explained Kirsty. 'I didn't want to resort to my usual remedy. I was saving that for when you came back.' And she went into the blue and white jar marked 'Flour' and took out her malt whisky.

Dad, Donald and Roderick had a wee dram in their tea. Archie and I celebrated with Coke while Kirsty phoned Jinty to tell her all was well.

Then we had to carry on with the normal routine of the inn as if nothing had happened.

That afternoon two couples arrived for bed and breakfast. They asked me what they should see while they were in Auchtertuie and I told them all about the walking, fishing, wildlife etc.

'This is such a lovely quiet place,' they said.

'Sometimes more goes on than you'd think,' I smiled.

The day was nearly done when Willie Ross's police car drew up outside the inn. All the other customers had gone and Dad, Roderick, Archie and I were the only ones left in the bar. Willie Ross came in. He was wearing his policeman's hat.

'Ah, Constable Ross,' said Dad. 'Did you have a good trip to Inverness?'

'I did,' said Constable Ross. 'But would you believe it, no sooner was my back turned than trouble breaks out at the big hotel.'

'You know about that already?' said Dad. 'I was going to report it to you in the morning. Our animals got loose again and somehow made their way through the estate to the hotel. The donkeys ate the flowers, the dogs got into the swimming pool, Flip was eating in the dining room and Emily scared the life out of Beachbabe. The hotel guests were very upset, but it wasn't the animals' fault, was it? How do you think they got out? Could it have been the same people as last time?'

Constable Ross stroked his chin. 'Very likely, I should think. First thing tomorrow, I shall be making a lot of enquiries at the hotel. They won't like it, you know. Apparently, having the police around is bad for business. But this *is* a bad business and I have to get to the bottom of it. I may have to search the entire hotel and the grounds. There will be a lot of disruption and inconvenience. I'm afraid some of the guests may leave.'

'That's too bad,' said Dad with a straight face.

'That's justice,' said Constable Ross, and left.

Chapter 29

I don't know who else Constable Ross had a word with, but I had a good idea. Next morning our local food supplies were restored. James Ross, the butcher, arrived in the kitchen with a big box of meat. He put it down on the table. Kirsty gave him a hostile look.

'And what can I do for you, Mr Ross?' she asked, in a voice that could have split sticks.

Archie and I, who'd been eating toast, stopped mid-munch, and Dad looked up from his bill-paying.

'I brought you some supplies.' James Ross was shamefaced. 'I just made a little mistake. Seems I had enough for you after all.'

'That's good, James,' said Dad.

GOOD! Was that all Dad was going to say!

I gave James Ross the scowl that even frightened me when I saw it in the mirror. 'I'm very pleased to hear you can still fit us in, Mr Ross. We do like to look after our customers.'

'Yes,' sniffed Kirsty. 'The same way we look after our friends.'

James Ross's florid face turned even pinker.

'I've ... er ... put in a couple of big roasts I won't be charging you for,' he said desperately. Then he escaped from the kitchen and the wrath of Kat and Kirsty McCrumble as fast as he could.

It was the same with Martin Murray from the fish van. But he wasn't brave enough to come into the kitchen, he just left a box of haddock and sea bass at the front door with a note: 'Sorry about the hiccup in supplies. Normal service now resumed. No charge for the enclosed.'

'I should think not,' said Kirsty, and rolled up her sleeves. 'Right, Kat, get out the blackboard and chalk and write out today's specials. Baked sea bass with a lime and garlic butter, haddock in a light beer batter with golden wonder chips, and Ross's rare roast à la Kirsty. Oh, and clootie dumpling for afters. That should bring people in.'

Kirsty was right. Lots of folks booked in for

dinner, and that night the inn was full to overflowing. Morag appeared to help Kirsty in the kitchen.

'I just knew you were going to be busy,' she said.

Roderick gave Dad a hand behind the bar and Archie and I helped serve the tables.

'I've never done this before,' said Archie. 'It's hard work.'

'Hard work never hurt anyone.' I mimicked Kirsty. 'And there's always the tips.'

We did really well that night and I went to bed tired, richer and a bit happier. I was happy that we had stood up to the crooks at the big hotel. Happy that we had turned the tables on them. I was still convinced that Ron Jackson was involved, though no doubt someone else had given him the orders. But I couldn't prove anything. I knew we'd need to be on the lookout for more dirty tricks, but, with Constable Ross taking a keen interest in what went on at the big hotel, I had a feeling we'd be safe for a while. That only left one problem. *We* might be safe, but Flip wasn't. There was still the big problem of the badger baiters. What were we going to do about them?

Chapter 30

Next day, after Archie and I had checked all the animals to see that they were none the worse for their adventure, we borrowed some waders and went fishing in Loch Bracken.

'This is fun,' said Archie, swaying a little as the current caught him. 'Do you do this often?'

'Nope, only when I want to get out of drying glasses. And we did enough of that yesterday to last us for a while.'

Archie nodded. 'Do you ever catch much out here?'

I shook my head. 'An occasional sea trout, but mostly empty drinks cans that stupid tourists throw in.'

'I think Samantha's hoping for a trout,' said Archie, nodding towards her.

Samantha had abandoned her usual tree in favour of a rock by the shore, and was giving us an expectant look.

'I'll do what I can,' I said. I'd used up nearly all her cat food for Flip.

I cast my line again. It snagged. Perhaps I had a bite. Was it a trout? Even a tiddler would do for Samantha. Nope. It was an old wellie. Samantha looked at me in disgust. She doesn't eat old wellies. She was just about to turn tail when Archie gave a yell. He had a bite. He lurched about, reeling in his line. Would you believe it, he had a small trout.

'Skill or what?' beamed Archie. 'Did you know that sea trout are migratory?'

I didn't. Neither did Samantha. Nor did she care. She tucked in daintily.

Archie and I sat on the rocks sunning ourselves while Samantha delicately licked her paws.

'I think she preferred that to cat food. Not like Flip,' he said.

'Speaking of Flip,' I said, 'I'm still really worried about the badger baiters. They won't lie low for long. We need to work out a plan to catch them. It could be Flip's sett next.'

'He didn't come for his food last night. Do you think he's all right?'

'Probably just tired and full up,' I said. 'But we can't take the chance. We'll have to organise a watch on the setts. This time we'll have to tell the dads or mine'll go bananas.'

'Mine too,' nodded Archie. 'He's already having enough trouble with Beachbabe. I'd better not add to it.'

'Is she still at the big hotel?' I was really curious, but hadn't liked to ask. Not like me, I know. Perhaps I was sickening for something.

'She's leaving for home today. Phoned Dad late last night with a big ultimatum. Either Dad did things her way or she was going back to the States and filing for divorce.'

'What happened?'

'She'll be halfway to Inverness airport by now.'

'Then what?'

Archie shrugged. 'He's been talking a lot about my mom recently, and she's asked to speak to him a couple of times when she's phoned me. For a change, it hasn't ended in a shouting match, so who knows?'

I gave him a friendly nudge with my elbow. 'Hey, maybe things'll work out.'

'Maybe,' said Archie.

Dad obviously felt the same way I did about the badger baiters for that night he called another 'family' meeting. Round the kitchen table were the usual suspects: Kirsty, Donald, Morag, Jinty, Roderick, Archie and me. Dad had also phoned Constable Ross, who metamorphosed into Willie when he took his hat off.

'You all know why we're here,' said Dad, 'and it's not just for Kirsty's scones.'

As usual the scones were piled high on a plate at one end of the table and a large tea pot stood ready. 'We must do something about the badger baiters. Certain people round this table tried to find them on their own, but that is too dangerous. What we need is a team effort.'

'Trouble is,' said Willie Ross, 'there is a huge area to cover, and at the moment there's only me to cover it. I've asked for extra police from Inverness, but it's holiday time and the force is stretched as it is, so, I'm afraid we'll just have to rely on each other.'

Everyone nodded their agreement and Archie's hand sneaked towards a scone.

'I think we should have teams,' I said, 'with someone on each team who knows the location of the badger setts. And I think we should all take our mobiles so we can keep in touch with each other. And I think we should carry a camera so we can have photographic evidence of what we see. And I think . . .'

'And I think you've thought about this, Kat,' smiled Willie Ross. 'But you're right. You are being very sensible.'

'See!' I smirked at Dad.

'There is a problem though,' said Donald, who'd sat quietly up till now. 'Even with two teams, and that's all it would be, for only Kat and I know the woods well enough, there are still a lot of setts to cover. Even if we don't count the ones that are pretty inaccessible.'

'That's true,' said Dad, 'but the alternative is to do nothing.'

'We can't do that,' I said quietly.

Everyone agreed, and as Kirsty poured out the tea, Dad spread out the big map and Donald and I pinpointed the badger setts.

'Each team can cover two setts in a night,' he said, 'but it's still a big task.'

'We can do it,' I said. 'Who's in my team?'

'Me,' said Archie.

'And me,' said Kirsty and Morag.

'That leaves me with Hector, Roderick and Jinty,' said Donald.

'Ah, wait now,' said Willie Ross. 'I don't think it's wise to leave the inn unattended after all that's happened. I think you should stay here, Hector.'

'Oh, but I can't. Perhaps Kirsty could stay instead.'

'No way,' said Kirsty. 'I missed out on the excitement last time. I'm going after these badger baiters. I'm going to give these criminals a piece of my mind, and the handle of my broom, if I get the chance.'

Finally Dad agreed, but turned to me and said, 'Just be careful, Kat. These men are dangerous. Don't do anything silly. Don't think you can take on the entire world on your own.'

'Me?' I squeaked. 'I don't think that.'

'Yes, you do,' grinned the others.

'Well,' I said, secretly pleased. 'Sometimes the world gets things so wrong it just has to be taken on, doesn't it?'

Chapter 31

We began that night. Donald's team took one side of the estate and mine the other. Morag drove us in her little post office van as close to our area as she could. We left the van in a lay-by and headed into the forest. It was exciting at first, trekking through the trees by moonlight, and we set off at a fair pace. But, as we got deeper and deeper into the forest, the going got tougher. The rain came on and we hunched our shoulders against it, though no matter how tightly I fastened my anorak hood, a little trickle of water still got in and ran down my neck.

'My boots are leaking,' muttered Archie.

I looked at his baseball boots. They weren't meant for forest trekking.

'And my socks are soggy,' he moaned.

'Welcome to Scotland in the summertime.'

We trudged on till we came to the sett we were looking for and hid among the trees. There was no sign of any badger baiters. After a while we moved on to the next sett and waited again. The forest settled down around us. As we grew still, the forest creatures grew bolder and resumed their nightly rituals. Voles and mice came out to forage. One of the mice came close enough to investigate my trailing bootlace. It tried a nibble but soon gave up. Rabbits came out to chew on the damp vegetation, and a fox slunk by, giving us a curious stare. Eyes blinked at us from time to time as deer wandered past. They seemed to know we meant them no harm. I wonder if animals can tell from your scent if you're friendly. It would be good if they could.

Despite the cold and damp, I felt my eyelids begin to droop.

Morag noticed.

'We'll take turns to watch,' she said. 'No point in all of us being awake.'

'Just don't snore,' I whispered to Archie as I closed my eyes.

I didn't sleep properly, just wandered in and out of strange dreams.

I came to with a start. I'd heard something. But it was just an owl calling to his mate.

When dawn started to appear, I shook the others.

'Time to go home,' I yawned. 'They won't come now.'

We trailed back through the forest to the lay-by where we'd left the van. By then, the morning air was crisp and fresh, and the sun was doing its best to dispel the sinister, black look of the loch. It was so quiet, I felt like we were the only humans left on the planet. We climbed into Morag's van and drove swiftly home along the empty winding road. Then Morag set off for work. I flopped on to my bed and fell into a deep sleep. It was so deep I didn't hear my alarm go off at 6.45 a.m., but I did hear the smoke alarm as Dad, in sole charge of breakfast, burnt the toast.

I got up and went downstairs. A bleary-eyed Donald had already reported that his team had had no luck the previous night either. I wandered about the kitchen half asleep till Morag appeared with the mail. She looked no better than me and fell asleep over the cup of tea I gave her. Her half-eaten scone fell from her hand and was promptly devoured by Max. Millie looked around for the odd crumb, but in vain. Max liked scones.

Kirsty was tired too. She was unusually quiet, and didn't even scold me for having a chocolate biscuit for my breakfast. Archie and Roderick were still in bed.

Help, I thought. If this is what we're like after only one night's badger watch, what are we going to be like a week from now?

Morag woke up with a start as tea spilled down her uniform trousers.

'Och, would you look at that?' she said. 'Now how did that happen . . .' Then she stopped and looked, not *at* me, but somehow *through* me. Her blue/brown eyes glazed over and took on their faraway look. She began to speak . . .

'I see the inn.'

Well, that was hardly strange, she was sitting in it.

'I see the forest . . .'

So could I, out of the window. Kirsty raised her eyes heavenwards. 'Maybe she's just fallen asleep again,' I said.

But she hadn't.

'I see little animals.' Morag smiled. 'They're playing together, rolling and tumbling over, having fun.'

'Badger cubs,' I said.

'There's a bigger animal gathering grass and

taking it into a hole in the ground.'

'Definitely badgers. That's Mum changing the beds.'

Then Morag's smile faded.

'It's darker now, but I see men and dogs. The dogs are straining at their leads. The men have lanterns. They're letting the dogs off the leads . . . oh, no!'

And Morag came back to us, her whole body trembling.

Kirsty quickly gave her some hot sweet tea.

'Sometimes this second sight is a curse,' whispered Morag, her face very pale. 'Sometimes I see terrible things.'

Kirsty put an arm round her shoulders and soothed her. 'There, there, Morag, it was those horrible badger baiters you saw. No wonder you're upset. They're on everybody's mind.'

I sat and watched as Millie gave Morag's hand a comforting lick and laid her head on her lap. My brain was working overtime. I went over and over what Morag had just said. The inn. The forest. The badgers. The dogs and the badger baiters. The inn. The forest. The badgers. The dogs and the badger baiters.

Then something went 'CLICK'. Morag had seen the badger baiters, not on the far side of the estate where we had expected them to be, but here in the forest, not far from the inn.

And whose sett was there?

Flip's.

Chapter 32

It was my turn to grow pale. We hadn't seen Flip since our visit to the big hotel.

'They could have got Flip!' I cried. I jumped up and ran out of the inn and across the yard. Donk gave me a startled look as I flew past. Millie and Max ran beside me, Kirsty and Morag at my heels.

'Kat, Kat,' they called. 'Wait for us.'

But I didn't. I dodged through the forest, leaping over tree-stumps, crashing through branches till I reached Flip's sett. All was quiet. No sign of any disturbance. No dead badgers. I prowled around. So did Millie and Max. There was still nothing unusual. I called the dogs to heel. For the first time, I noticed it was raining hard. There was a noise behind me and a panting Kirsty and Morag appeared at my side.

'They haven't been yet,' I said. 'The sett's not been disturbed and there's no sign of the ground being trampled. Perhaps Flip's just staying at home because he senses danger.'

'Well, you're in danger too if you don't get home right now, Katriona McCrumble,' grumbled Kirsty. 'Gave Morag and me the fright of our lives, taking off like that. We haven't run so fast since we won the three-legged race at the Auchtertuie Games.'

'Danger?' I asked.

'Of catching your death of cold. Next time you run off, kindly make sure you are wearing more than a pair of flowery pink pyjamas and one slipper.'

'Oh.' I looked down. 'I expect I'll find the other slipper on the way back.'

'Here you are, Cinderella,' grinned Morag, and held it up. 'If the slipper fits, you shall go to the ball, you shall marry Prince Archie.'

'Archie?' I squeaked. 'You have to be kidding. He's just a friend who happens to be a boy, that's all. He never thinks of ME as his girlfriend.'

'I know someone else who's like that,' said Morag sadly. 'Come on, let's go home.'

Dad was pacing the floor when we got back.

'So there you are,' he said, looking really cross. 'Where on earth were you? I came back with the morning papers to find you all gone, and the inn as deserted as the *Mary Celeste*. There's half-eaten food on the table and the back door is wide open . . .'

'There, there, Hector,' soothed Kirsty. 'No need to worry. We're all just fine. Now sit yourself down while I put on the kettle. Kat will tell you the story.'

This was getting to be a habit.

'Well,' I said. 'It started with Morag and her second sight . . .'

Dad raised his eyes heavenwards. 'Make mine a large mug of tea, Kirsty. This sounds like a long tale.'

And a scary one.

But Dad was sceptical. 'I think it's unlikely the badger baiters would come so close to the inn,' he said. 'They're more likely, as we first thought, to keep as far away as possible.'

'I'm sorry, Hector,' sniffed Morag. 'But I see what I see. I can't change that.'

Dad patted her hand. 'I know, but I don't think . . .'

'I don't think we can take the chance,' I said. 'One team will have to keep an eye on Flip's sett and I volunteer mine.'

'OK,' Dad agreed readily.

Too readily, I thought. He probably reckoned I'd be safer guarding Flip's sett.

I went upstairs and changed out of my damp pyjamas. By the time I got back to the kitchen Archie and Roderick had appeared and were wolfing down bacon and eggs. They really had become part of the family.

'Being out in the middle of the night certainly gives you an appetite,' smiled Roderick.

Archie nodded, but for once said nothing. His mouth was too full.

While they ate I told them about our change of plan. Like Dad, Roderick was sceptical.

'I don't know, Kat,' he said. 'Some of your Scottish ways are surely strange to me, but I thought our first plan was a sound one.'

'But you didn't see Morag,' I said. 'She was so upset at what she saw and she's been right before.'

'And wrong,' murmured Kirsty.

I nodded. 'But with Flip and his family we just can't take the chance.'

And Morag wasn't the only one who 'saw' things that day either.

I spent most of the day helping Dad with the new guests. The inn was full of people coming and going all the time, and Kirsty could hardly make cakes fast enough to cope with the demand for morning coffees and afternoon teas. At one point, I thought I might have to make my celebrated fairy cakes, but Kirsty declined my offer of help.

'You stick to looking after the animals, Kat. That's what you're really good at.'

'OK,' I agreed, and skipped out to chat to Donk.

He was a little bit sad. Lily's owners had come back from their holidays and taken her home.

'I'm sorry, old fellow,' I said, stroking his ears. 'I know you're a bit lonely now. I know you like Lily, but her human family like her too, and want to have her with them. I promise, one of these days, when we have a bit more money, we'll get another friend for you.'

Donk nuzzled my ear. I hoped he understood.

We still had Emily with us, and Seamus and Brandy and Ginger. I visited all of them and had a chat. Archie found me trying to brush Seamus's shaggy coat.

'I've brushed it and brushed it,' I said. 'But it still doesn't look any better.'

'Some folks are just naturally scruffy,' said Archie, looking at my mud-stained jeans and holey jumper.

'Would you rather I looked like Beachbabe?' I asked.

Archie shuddered. 'Actually, I came out here to look for you. I have some news.'

'About Beachbabe?'

'About my mom. She's coming over to see me and Dad. Seems they've been talking quite a bit on the phone.'

'Do you think they might get back together?'

'Who knows?' shrugged Archie. 'Parents are from another planet, but I do know Dad's been really cheerful since he heard. Can't stop singing.'

'That's good.'

'You haven't heard him sing.'

There was singing in the bar that night. It was really busy because Angus McDowall, the fiddler, was in. Angus is about ninety-four . . . he thinks. He has a face like a brown elf, wispy white hair and long bony fingers that fly over his fiddle like lightning. The customers love his music. Angus started off with some Scottish reels. People began clapping, then toes started tapping, and before you could say hairy haggis there was an eightsome reel whirling round the bar. More folks joined in and the dancing spilled out on to the street. Before long, locals and visitors alike were having a ceilidh. That often happens when Angus starts to play.

I left them to it and ran upstairs to get ready to

watch over Flip's sett. At the top of the stairs a figure was waiting for me. I nearly bumped into him, if you can bump into a ghost. I stopped abruptly. Old Hamish smiled. I smiled back. Then Old Hamish grew anxious and agitated.

'What is it, Hamish?' I asked. 'What's the matter?'

Old Hamish hovered along to the end of the corridor. I followed. He stopped by the window and pointed out.

'The back yard,' I said.

Old Hamish shook his head.

'Donk and the dogs?'

Old Hamish shook his head again.

'The forest?'

Old Hamish nodded.

'The badgers?'

Old Hamish nodded so hard I thought his head might fall off.

'It's tonight, isn't it?'

Old Hamish nodded again and put a hand on my arm. I felt no weight, only a slight chill.

Then he disappeared, and I had no doubt that the hand on my arm was Old Hamish telling me to be careful.

Chapter 33

I didn't get the chance to tell Dad about Old Hamish, he was so busy in the bar. But I did whisper it to the rest of my team as we made our way through the forest to Flip's sett.

'It's a sign,' Morag whispered back.

Then the four of us trudged on in silence. The sett was about a kilometre away. When we got near, I motioned the others to stop as I crept forward to have a look. Flip's sett was in a little clearing among the trees. I could see what I thought was the main entrance, but knew there would be many others. I knew that the entire area was lined with tunnels, knew that there was a whole badger city beneath my feet.

At first there was no movement, and we just waited and waited. Then a black and white striped head popped out of the sett, and Flip, followed by Mrs Flip and two little cubs, came out to play. Flip sniffed the air. Could he scent me or was there something else? We sat very quietly and watched the badgers play for a while. Then Flip's head lifted and he grew still. Something had alerted him. I listened hard, but could hear nothing. But Flip wasn't happy. He ushered Mrs Flip and the cubs back into the sett and followed them inside. Not long after, from quite far off, came a faint scuffling and some tiny pinpoints of light. The scuffling and lights drew closer.

'It's them,' whispered Morag. 'It's just like I saw earlier. It's them.'

I was sick with nerves. Archie's eyes grew luminous. Morag and Kirsty were moonlight pale.

'Phone Willie Ross right now, Kat,' whispered Kirsty. 'This is police business.'

I took out my mobile and tried to make contact. Nothing. What was wrong with this phone! I gave it a thump. Still nothing. The others tried their phones too. Useless. There was obviously no signal in this part of the forest. There was no way we could get help quickly, and the badger baiters were coming closer and closer. What could we do?

I thought fast.

'Sing,' I hissed to the others.

'What?' hissed Archie back. 'Flip's family are about to be torn apart and you want us to party?'

'We can't stop men with dogs. We don't know how many there are, so we have to try to scare them off. Perhaps they'll think we're revellers from the inn.'

'What shall we sing?' asked Morag.

' "Mhairi's wedding".'

'I don't know the words,' said Archie.

'Then dance, make a noise, do something. Improvise!'

'Step we gaily on we go,' started Kirsty.

I winced and joined in. Kirsty had a voice like a flattened frog.

'Heel for heel and toe for toe,' sang Morag, in a voice that had come close to winning the Mod.

'Hooch aye, the noo,' yelled Archie.

I winced again. What Scottish programmes had that boy been watching?

But he did his best. He pranced about like a rodeo horse and made a noise like a constipated bull.

The lights grew brighter as they drew nearer.

'Surely they must have heard us,' I sang.

'Half the country must have heard us,' sang Kirsty.

'Arm in arm and row on row,' ploughed on Morag.

'All for Mhairi's wedding,' we all joined in.

More lights appeared.

'They're still coming towards us,' I despaired. 'Our singing hasn't worked.'

Suddenly there were voices. Loud men's voices. And barking. Loud excited barking. And four men, with terriers at their heels, ran through the trees straight for us.

'Right.' Kirsty pushed up her sleeves.

'Och, I wish I'd done a course in karate instead of flower arranging,' wailed Morag.

Archie looked around for a stick and I . . . well, my McCrumble temper just rose and rose and I got really, really angry. I broke cover and ran out across the clearing towards the men. 'You miserable cowards,' I yelled. 'Don't you come anywhere near these badgers. Go and pick on someone your own size!'

But it made no difference. The lights were almost upon us now and the badger baiters ran towards me. I could see they wore heavy boots, camouflage clothing and balaclavas. Their dogs snapped around their heels. But I was too fired up to be afraid.

'Stop!' I yelled. 'Stop!' But they charged right up to me and . . . past me. 'What?'

Then I saw why. Hard on their heels was Constable Ross with Dad, Donald, Roderick and some of the Auchtertuie McCrumbles. Millie and Max were there too. Max was thoroughly excited, he thought this was a great game.

But the badger baiters weren't giving up easily. They crashed on through the forest and might have escaped . . . if they hadn't run into an ambush. As if by magic, more McCrumbles suddenly appeared from behind nearby trees.

'How? What? Where did they all come from?' I gasped. But my words were lost among the bloodcurdling yells of Lachy, Mario, Luigi and others, who brought the badger baiters down with some highly illegal rugby tackles. Constable Ross's group joined in the fray, and the badger baiters, who were vastly outnumbered, were soon overpowered. Half the village, it seemed, had turned out to help catch them.

The villagers grinned as they marched the badger baiters out of the forest, down Auchtertuie's main street, to the tiny police station. Constable Ross's jail cell had never been so full. He took charge of the badger baiters and we took charge of their dogs. We led them back to the inn, fed them, and bedded them down in an empty pen. It wasn't their fault they'd been trained to do dirty work.

I couldn't believe what had taken place. It had all happened so quickly. But I was grinning all over my face. So was my dad. But he had some explaining to do. In the wee small hours, when we were all back round the kitchen table, he told us what happened . . .

'It was old Angus McDowall that alerted me,' said Dad. 'He said a man had come, supposedly from me, and given him money, to play in the bar. Now Angus never takes money for his playing. He says, what would a man of his age want with money? So, I was suspicious, and when Angus said he thought the man was "yon mouthy gamekeeper from the estate", I was doubly suspicious. I thought maybe, *maybe*, Morag was right and Angus was being used to create a diversion to keep us busy. So I phoned Willie Ross and he thought it a possibility too. We put the word round and Willie gathered a McCrumble posse, half of which came with us, and half sneaked up behind you. Donald took us by another route into the forest, and we watched out for the bad guys.'

'I tried to call for help,' I said, 'but my phone wouldn't work. It's lucky you were all there.'

'Oh, I don't know,' grinned Dad. 'That singing was pretty awful. Nearly scared US off.'

Then he gave me a big hug that said I love you,

and I gave him a big one back. He's a nice man, my dad, and quite smart sometimes, even if he can't make decent toast.

Next day, the local paper was full of what had happened, and just about everybody in Auchtertuie, including Ali McAlly with his teeth in, had their photographs on the front page. It was a good likeness of Dad, but I looked like something Samantha had dragged in.

'Good photo of you, Kat,' grinned Archie.

I would have thumped him, but I was in too good a mood. Constable Ross had phoned to say there was a little reward due to me for all my work in helping to catch the badger baiters. And I knew exactly what I was going to do with it.

'What?' asked Dad.

'Buy a friend for Donk. He really misses Lily.'

'That won't be necessary,' smiled Dad. 'I've just spoken to Lily's owners. Apparently she really misses Donk too and has been pining ever since she went home. They want to know if they can board Lily with us permanently. She'll be back with us soon.'

'Fantastic,' I said. 'Then we can put the reward money towards the wildlife sanctuary.'

'Oh, I think you deserve to spend a little of the money on yourself,' said Dad.

'OK.' I didn't take a lot of persuading. 'But what'll I get?'

'How about some new jeans, sweaters, haircut, singing lessons . . . ?' said Archie.

I thumped him. But gently. He was one of the good guys.

Chapter 34

The next night we had a ceilidh at the inn to celebrate. Just about everyone was there. Lots of people came in kilts and Roderick was delighted. He and Archie appeared in their McCrumble tartan trews.

'I know,' I grinned at Archie. 'You just want to blend in!'

But that gave me an idea. I raced upstairs and dived into my wardrobe. I had a little tartan number as well. The painting competition I had won had been to design an up-to-date tartan outfit. I had drawn a little white cropped top, caught at one shoulder with a McCrumble tartan ribbon, and a hipster McCrumble tartan mini-kilt. Kirsty and

Morag had made it up for me as a surprise after I had won the competition. I had never worn it, until now. I put it on, pulled my hair up in a heavy silver clasp that had been my mum's and went downstairs.

In the hall, Angus McDowall was frenziedly fiddling, and Archie was being twirled from arm to arm by Kirsty and Morag in a vigorous Dashing White Sergeant. Archie saw me. His eyes opened wide, his mouth opened wide and he missed Morag's outstretched arm. He fell at my feet.

Perhaps I should wear this little number more often!

'Cool outfit, Kat,' he grinned.

'I just want to blend in too,' I grinned back, and joined in the fun.

I had a great evening. So did Morag. She danced a slow Scottish waltz round the lounge with Dad, and her eyes took on that faraway look. But I don't think it had anything to do with the second sight. Willie Ross appeared in his kilt and did a sword dance. He was amazingly light on his feet, despite his size twelves. He whispered to Dad that he didn't think he could prove anything against Ron Jackson, but that he'd be keeping a close eye on him. I kept a close eye on Max, who was trying to steal everyone's crisps.

Towards the end of the evening, I went out to see

Donk. It was a fine night and he was scratching the side of his head against the fence post. I scratched the other side for him. Then Archie appeared.

'I thought I'd find you here,' he said, and handed me a Coke.

He looked around at the old inn, at its old stone walls streaked with pink and gold from the setting sun.

'I've had a great time here, Kat,' he said. 'I didn't realise when Dad said we were coming to visit the place of his ancestors that I'd have so many adventures.'

I smiled and stroked Donk's odd-shaped nose. 'Auchtertuie's a surprising place,' I said. 'But, I expect America is too. I may just have to come and check it out sometime.'

'Anytime,' grinned Archie. 'But, meantime, once I've gone home, you will keep in touch, won't you? You will phone me and tell me what's been happening here?'

'Of course,' I said, as Donk nuzzled my ear.

And, I may not have Morag's second sight, but I had a sudden funny feeling that my dad might start complaining about the size of his phone bill.

Tooth-rotting recipe overleaf →

Recipe for Tablet

Go on, try it, and try not to eat it all yourself.

This is the author's recipe (there are lots of others). Please ask an adult for help when making this recipe, because the ingredients get very hot.

4oz (100g) butter
2¼ lbs (1kg) sugar
6 fl.oz (0.2l) whole milk
1 large tin of condensed milk

- Gently melt butter in large saucepan. Ask an adult to help and always be very careful with hot pans.
- Add sugar and milk and stir till sugar has dissolved.
- Add condensed milk and bring mixture slowly to the boil. Let it simmer gently for about 20 minutes.
- With the help of an adult, take off heat and beat with a wooden spoon for about five minutes or until your arm drops off.
- Pour into a shallow dish and mark into fingers before the tablet sets.
- Enjoy!